Oil
OF
Joy

May 2008

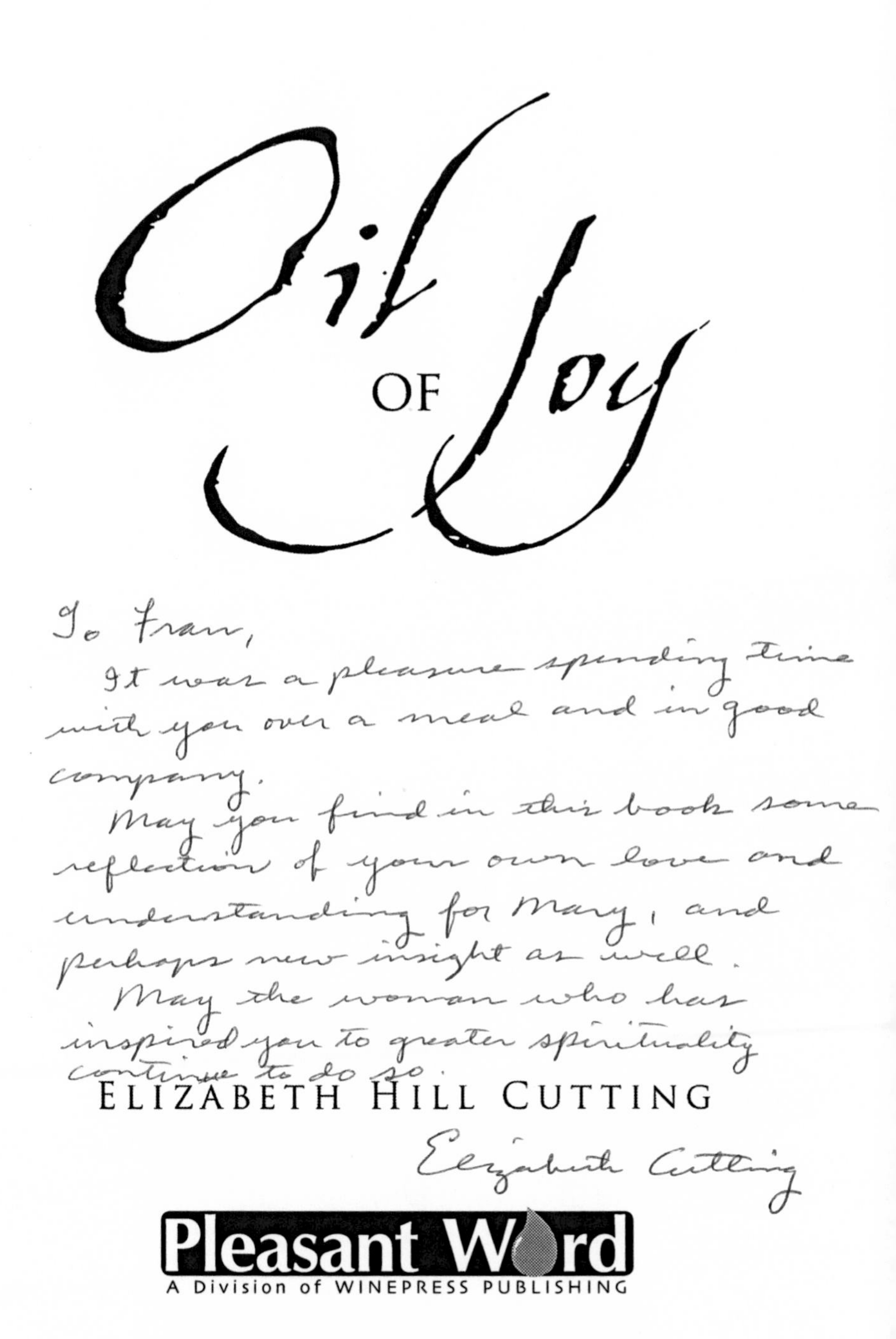

Oil of Joy

To Fran,
It was a pleasure spending time with you over a meal and in good company.
May you find in this book some reflection of your own love and understanding for Mary, and perhaps new insight as well.
May the woman who has inspired you to greater spirituality continue to do so.

ELIZABETH HILL CUTTING

Elizabeth Cutting

Pleasant Word
A Division of WINEPRESS PUBLISHING

Pleasant Word (a division of WinePress Publishing, PO Box 428, Enumclaw, WA 98022) functions only as book publisher. As such, the ultimate design, content, editorial accuracy, and views expressed or implied in this work are those of the author.

ISBN 1-4141-0613-0
Library of Congress Catalog Card Number: 2005909813

"The Spirit of the Lord God is upon me,
because the Lord has anointed me...
to grant to those who mourn...
the oil of gladness instead of mourning ...

—Isa. 61:1,3.

Dedication

To my mother, Anna Elizabeth Viehweg Hill.

She has been an inspiration to me, and to others, because of her abiding faith in God's leading in her life.

Table of Contents

Acknowledgement

I would like to thank Congregation B'nai Israel in Muskegon, Michigan, for the use of their library for the purposes of research.

Chapter One

Anticipation

"I hope Mary knows what she's doing. My Nathan says she's being very foolish to go to Jerusalem right now."

As Mary approached the small stream where the village women did their laundry, she heard Judith, one of her neighbors, speak these words. She stopped, hoping Judith would elaborate on Nathan's statement.

"I know," agreed another voice, which Mary also recognized. It was Rebekah, wife of the innkeeper and someone she always considered a friend. "We had a caravan from that direction stop by the inn last night. They wanted to get to Zippori before evening, but it got too late. They had to settle for little old Nazareth. But anyway, where was I? Oh yes, Zadok had asked one of the men about Jesus, as he does every time anyone comes into town. He was always fond of him and likes to know where he is and what he's doing. He's so ashamed that Jesus can't feel welcome and comfortable in his own hometown anymore, to say nothing of wishing he could see him again himself and talk with him as he used to do until three years ago."

Judith, impatient that Rebekah might ramble away from the subject as she was prone to do, demanded, "What did he say—this man from Jerusalem?"

"He hadn't seen him. Jesus doesn't stay anywhere for long, you know. But he certainly had heard some strange things. It seems Jesus has got the whole Sanhedrin in a dither. One of the drivers told Zadok all kinds of things that he's heard about a man named Jesus."

"What kinds of things?" Judith asked.

"It seems he's causing the temple authorities problems over matters like working on the Sabbath, forgiving sins, religious authority—things like that. You know Jesus' reputation for healing people. Sometimes it happens to be a Sabbath day when he heals. That's upsetting in itself to the scribes and Pharisees. Even worse, though, according to this driver, Jesus has been heard to tell people their sins have been forgiven. And as if that isn't bad enough—this may not have been true since the caravaneer had been drinking much wine and could have been addle-headed…"

"What, what?" Judith grew impatient with Rebekah's conversational side trips.

"Sorry. The caravaneer said something about Jesus raising a man from the dead, a man who had been in his tomb already several days."

"Oh, my! That must be what Nathan was thinking about. When he came back from Jerusalem last week, he said that Jesus had gone too far. The chief priests and the Pharisees have decided something drastic needs to be done before he causes real damage. They are afraid people will reject their faith to follow a magician who can take away all their troubles in some strange and supernatural way."

Mary could stand it no longer. "Good morning, Judith, Rebekah."

She walked toward the water and thumped her clothes basket down on the ground. As she dipped a garment into the water and began vigorously rubbing it, she asked, "How does Nathan know of this decision?"

Rebekah and Judith looked at each other sheepishly.

Eyes downcast, Judith said, "Mary, I'm sorry. We didn't know you were there."

"I'm sure of that, and I know you both well enough to know that you are only concerned for me. But I mean to go to Jerusalem tomorrow. It is too important to me to stay home because of a few rumors."

"Well, maybe it is just rumors," Judith conceded.

"I am positive that's all it is," Mary stated vehemently.

She continued, "I still want to know what makes Nathan so sure the things he heard are truth and not rumor, that the chief priests want to take measures against Jesus. What authority do those have who told him this?"

Judith responded. "When Nathan finished selling his loomed linen cloth in the bazaar, he went to the temple as usual. It's such an exciting place for him, so different from quiet little Nazareth—so many people coming and going—so much happening there all the time, and news from all over. Anyway, he walked over to the Royal Porch so he could listen to the rabbis teaching. On the other side of one of the columns he heard some Pharisees talking and stopped when he heard Jesus' name. Even though they tried to control their voices, he could still hear the agitation. And they said these things—that something had to be done about Jesus."

"Well, maybe it's all just talk," Rebekah offered. "After all, what can they do but reprimand him if they think he's gone beyond the bounds of religious acceptability? He hasn't done anything that would deserve punishment, I'm sure. He isn't a murderer or a blasphemer. He's done only good things that help people. The problem is, though, that our religious leaders do have the last word, and they obviously consider his behavior improper."

"Do you think he behaves improperly?" Mary directed her gaze first at the one, then the other, watching their faces for any flicker of the real truth of what they thought.

Judith and Rebekah were obviously uncomfortable. Mary knew they wished they hadn't been so outspoken in such a public place, and that they didn't want to hurt her feelings, especially not Rebekah. She and Zadok had been very good to her family following Joseph's death. Zadok had taken upon himself a measure of responsibility for Jesus, who as a teenager had suddenly found himself head of a household. Zadok's counsel had been welcome as well as helpful.

"Well, we've never seen him do any of these things we hear about," Judith hedged, "so maybe it's just exaggeration by people who are jealous of his popularity. We can't really judge for ourselves because here in Nazareth we have only what he said in synagogue when he visited that once..." Her voice trailed off to nothing because she had said too much once again. Inadvertently she had brought up a subject that would be painful to Mary.

"Yes," Mary murmured mournfully. "That's all we in Nazareth have." She thought, *Jesus was right when he said, "A prophet is not without honor except in his own country." Everywhere else the wonders of his special work are known, people are healed, but not here in Nazareth.*

Rebekah and Judith had finished their laundry. Mary knelt, vehemently beating a garment with a small laundering club. She rid herself of the anger and frustration that had been rising within her even more than she rid the cloth of any dirt that might lurk there. Rebekah walked over to Mary, took her elbow, and lifted her to her feet. Embracing her, she said, "I'm sorry. I'm sorry for all that you have endured, and I'm sorry for any additional pain I may have caused you. Go in peace to Jerusalem, and God go with you." As she spoke, she tightened her hug.

Mary responded to the embrace, saying with tears in her voice, "Thank you, Rebekah. And don't fret; all will be well. I know it in my heart."

Judith joined them, saying, "You are fortunate to be celebrating Passover in Jerusalem. I too am sorry for my rash words. Please forgive me, and go in peace." Then the two women left Mary alone with the remainder of her laundry and her troubled thoughts.

Mary mentally rehashed all that had just been said, all that she had heard before, and all that she herself knew to be true. She realized that whatever anyone said, there was truth in all of it. The chief priests and the scribes and the Pharisees were unhappy, no doubt about it. But she could give no place to fear because Jesus was doing what he had been born to do. What a pity that the Nazarenes could not have experienced Jesus' healing and teaching.

They had nothing except Jesus' words, the words he used to proclaim that God had sent him to them. Who could forget those words? Everyone was so proud of Jesus in that moment, a young man from their own hometown, called by God to care for them—to heal them, to aid the poor among them, to release them from the bondage of Rome. What a glorious moment. Then in an instant Jesus turned it all upside down. His next words implied that the Gentiles would receive these gifts.

The congregation understood that the Jews were in covenant with God. If any people should have God's blessings, it was the Jews—not the pagan Gentiles. The healing ministry of the anointed one was for them. Isaiah couldn't have meant anything else. It was such abomination to all the people gathered there that they turned against him in hot anger. They would have killed him had he not miraculously escaped from their grasp as they pushed him toward the brow of a steep hill.

The memory of those awful moments rekindled the fear and the sorrow that she felt at that time. It had not been easy living in Nazareth these three years, knowing what the villagers had tried to do to Jesus. She had done her best to heed her son's advice to forgive those who hurt her. At the same time she appreciated those who had remained loyal to her family, especially Judith and Nathan, Rebekah and Zadok.

Because of that day, she thought, *Jesus has not been back to Nazareth to do any of his wonderful works among those who watched him grow up, watched him become a fine young man. How sad this is for all of us.*

Mary labored on, soaping her clothes, beating them, rinsing them, expelling anger along with the soil. As she worked, she felt calmer. Her thoughts turned to that day long ago before she was even married. She knew she had more than mere words. She had a promise, a promise from God himself. Gabriel, angel of the Lord God, had come to her to tell her she was to have his Son, a special child to whom the Lord would give the throne of his ancestor David, and he would reign forever. She wasn't sure how Jesus' work and the throne of David had anything to do with each other. But she knew the angel was truthful, and she knew God would keep his word. He would not let anything happen to Jesus. No matter what anyone said or believed, Jesus could not be prevented from doing the work God sent him to do, not even by the Sanhedrin itself.

Having completed her task, Mary picked up the basket, heavier now than when she had come to the stream, but her footsteps were as light as they had been before she overheard Rebekah and Judith. She was not going to let their idle gossip, derived from rumors, spoil her anticipation of what lay ahead.

When Mary reached home, she hurried up the outside steps to the roof and hung her clean laundry over the wall to dry. She knew it would take less than an hour, and then she could pack it away for her journey. She hurried downstairs and put into the oven the loaves she had set to rise early that morning, then set about gathering the food that she would take to eat along with her bread—dried fruit, olives, cheese, and some thin wine in a leather wineskin.

As she put it all into a small covered basket, she thought about how she would pass the remainder of the day. She knew she would have to rest in the afternoon. She would be tired from the morning's work. Besides, she could accomplish nothing in the midday heat. After her rest she would see Jonathan to find out exactly what time he intended to leave the following morning and to pay him the final amount owed for the journey.

Then she would go to James' house where all the other children and their families would be gathered to share the evening meal together, to wish her a safe journey, and to plead with her one more time not to go. Yes, that would be part of it because they had not lost any opportunity to try to dissuade her from the journey. That thought brought a pang of pain back into her heart. It wasn't just other people in Nazareth who had rejected Jesus; it was also his own family. She knew he had been painfully aware of that fact because when he said a prophet wasn't honored in his own country, he had also added, not even in his own home.

James, Joseph, Simon, and Judas, and their sisters had been embarrassed by Jesus' reputation and had reacted negatively in varying degrees. They had tried, especially James, to reason with him, to badger him, somehow to get him to give up his wanderings, his itinerant teaching. They too had heard the rumors from the south and were quite certain that Jesus was moving toward his own destruction. If Mary, their mother, went to Jerusalem and joined him there, she would also be in danger.

But I can't give it up, she thought. *I have planned this for so long. I want nothing more than to be able to spend a little time with my eldest son whom I see too seldom. No, no matter what they say, I will not be put off.*

She had no way to know of the terror she would face in one week's time.

Chapter Two

Coronation

The hot dusty travelers sprawled on the roadside. Judas massaged his foot, sore from the irritation of a pebble that had worked its way between his toes. The pebble had been annoying enough, but it wasn't the whole source of his discomfort. His mental state was becoming increasingly agitated and all the more because he could not speak of it to anyone. With every step of this fifteen-mile walk from Jericho, he had become more deeply troubled.

Every time they had passed a Roman watchtower, he had fumed inwardly. These stone sentinels were a mockery, dotting the landscape of the homeland of an occupied people. Judas knew he had to take some kind of action—and soon. He had already lost three years following the man whom he had thought would be the leader Judea needed. But Jesus apparently didn't understand the situation as Judas did.

Somehow he had to do something to make up for the precious time he had lost following Jesus about, and now he had determined what he would do. While they were in Jerusalem, he would find some opportunity to convince Jesus that Judas' ideas were right, to make him see that the course he was pursuing was wrong. He hadn't formulated any definite plan, but at least he had made the difficult decision to force Jesus' hand while he was still popular.

As they had moved from the heat and starkness of the wilderness around Jericho to the arboreal fullness of the richly cultivated fields and vineyards of Jerusalem, he remembered how much he had hoped the same kind of transformation would occur in the lives of his countrymen. Judas had committed himself to the task of bringing about this transformation, the bringing in of a new age of freedom for his people. He had been enthusiastic about Jesus because he had seen in him hope for the fulfillment of the dream, the dream of independence forevermore.

His desire to associate himself with Jesus, whose ideas about the kingdom of God seemed to mesh with his own ideas of the new age, was sincere. To Judas the kingdom meant sovereignty of the Hebrew nation, and it would be brought about by the Messiah. Some had been convinced early that the Messiah had come in the person of Jesus, and so it seemed to Judas as he observed his supernatural power at work and his popularity with the people. He knew that Jesus could become king of Judea if he made even the least effort because the people adored him.

But Jesus has done nothing, he fumed inwardly, *nothing in three whole years, to take control!* He had shown no inclination to take kingly power. He healed the sick; he told stories; he spent his time with people who had no political influence. Judas believed that the bringing in of the new age of political independence for his beloved Hebrew nation required a fully dedicated effort, which Jesus was not making. He had hoped that this would be forthcoming, that Jesus would soon become actively engaged in acquiring his kingly position.

In the meantime Judas had been content to participate fully as a disciple, going out with the others to preach and to heal, and the experience had exhilarated him. He had come to love the Master, and because of this love his present confusion about Jesus' mission tore at his soul. He had somehow become two separate persons: one Judas desiring the companionship of his Master and friends, the other Judas hating Jesus for misleading him.

For some weeks now the dark, hating side of Judas had been thinking of methods he could use to perhaps get Jesus to change his ways. This inward battle, which led to the decision that he would oppose Jesus if he didn't soon begin to lead a revolt, caused him so much agitation.

Now that they were in Bethphage, not far from Jerusalem, it wouldn't be long before he could speak to someone about the possibilities for some kind of action. As they neared the Golden City, he heard rumors about the Sanhedrin putting out WANTED posters all over Jerusalem, hoping someone would bring Jesus to them.

Yes, he thought, *that gives me an idea. I'll speak to someone on the Council. They will certainly be happy to see me. They have been angry and upset about Jesus for a long time now.*

Having decided this, Judas questioned anew the wisdom of this man. Jesus, like Judas, knew what was happening in Jerusalem, and that he would surely be arrested if he entered the city, yet he was determined to go there. *The man is a fool, no doubt about it, and I'm no longer going to follow a fool.* There! His course was set. It was time to take matters into his own hands.

"How's your foot, Judas?" Thaddaeus broke into Judas' heavy, dark thoughts. Judas momentarily could not speak, so far back was he in the shadowed corners of his mind. When he did speak, it was as though from far way.

"Oh, it's all right now. I'm ready to move on. I'm sure the Master is anxious to reach Jerusalem."

"You left us for a time. It seemed as though you were a long way away. Care to share your thoughts?" Thaddaeus offered.

Swallowing a sip of water from the water pouch the men passed around, Judas slowly responded, "I was just thinking about Jesus… and the meaning of messiahship."

"That *is* heavy thinking all right."

The others began to rise, anxious to end the journey, but Jesus raised his hand to stay them.

"Philip. Andrew. Go into Bethphage where you will find a donkey tied to a doorpost, along with her colt. Untie them both and bring them here to me. If anyone questions your action, tell them, 'The Lord needs them immediately.'"

Philip and Andrew rose to do as they were told while the others murmured among themselves, wondering if Jesus was too tired to walk farther. He had seemed very tired and depressed of late, nor was he joyously anticipating their return to Jerusalem. Something was different this time.

As Philip and Andrew left, Philip worried, "How are we to walk away with someone else's animals? We'll be branded for theft or forced to drive a grain-mill wheel."

Andrew replied, "Well, it does seem to be a strange request, but I'm sure the Master knows what he is about. He wouldn't ask us to do it if it were wrong."

Since they had been just outside the limits of Bethphage, a small village, only a few minutes passed before they saw two donkeys tied to a doorpost by the roadway. Andrew went and untied them. As he did, a man standing a little distance away ran toward them, shouting, "What are you doing with my animals?"

Andrew turned, facing a man ready to fight for his property if need be. Sounding more confident than he felt, he said, "The Lord needs them immediately."

To their amazement the man relaxed and nodded, his eyes brightening. Waving his hand, he said to them, "Go, then, in peace."

Upon their return they shared with the others how it had all happened just as Jesus said it would.

When the two brought the animals to Jesus, the disciples spread their garments on the foal's back for him to sit on, and they started toward Jerusalem.

News must have spread ahead of them. As they descended the Mount of Olives, people ran out to meet them, strewing palm branches all over the road in front of Jesus. Some even threw their garments on the roadway for Jesus to pass over. And they waved palm branches ahead of him, heralding his approach.

"Hosanna in the highest. Hosanna! Hosanna! Hosanna to the Son of David! Blessed be he who comes in the name of the Lord. Blessed be the kingdom of our father David that is coming!" The sounds of a jubilant multitude pierced the air. "Hosanna! Blessed be the king who comes in the name of the Lord! Peace in heaven and glory in the highest! Hosanna! Hosanna! The king, the son of David, comes in the name of the Lord! Hosanna! Hosanna!"

It was a joyous time, the celebration so contagiously tumultuous that it drew in more and more people. Otherwise disinterested people, who had been occupied with their daily business routines, had their curiosity aroused. They also began to follow along.

Nearly everyone caught up in this joyful drama believed that Jesus was the king due their allegiance. He had come to them in peace on a donkey, a baby donkey, not on a mighty stallion as to war. He would bring peace to their troubled nation. He would make things right without war, without bloodshed and death. What's more, he was a king who cared about them as he would his own children. He healed their illnesses, calmed their fears, raised their dead. Hadn't Lazarus been dead four days, and he brought him back to life? Some of these who now heralded Jesus had been there and seen it with their own eyes. Others had heard and wanted to believe the unbelievable. This was the king for them.

"Hosanna! Blessed be our king!"

Judas could hardly believe what he witnessed. Here he had given up completely, was even ready to turn his teacher over to the Council, and now this. Maybe he hadn't been patient enough. Jesus entered the city as any king would who came in peace. Maybe these three years had been necessary to allow people to know who he was in order to ensure his position. The multitudes, the very people Judas had believed had no political influence, glorified him, totally accepting his royal status. Surely now Jesus would take measures to expel Rome from Judea, to stop the defilement of their country by these heathen tyrants. But he had had his hopes up before only to have them dashed. He would just have to wait and see. Whatever happened in the next couple of days would decide it. Then Judas would know whether Jesus was indeed a worthy king of the Jews—or a fraud.

"Teacher! Teacher!" A Pharisee, wearing the bleached linen tunic that proclaimed humility, called for the attention of the man on the donkey. The roar of the crowd diminished somewhat as the strident voice intruded on their revelry and the speaker was able to make himself heard. "Teacher, rebuke your disciples. Don't you hear what they are saying?"

"I tell you," Jesus countered, "if these were silent, the very stones would soon cry out." Yes, the time had come. The king must be announced, if not by these children of Judah, then by nature herself for she would be compelled to burst forth with the happy proclamation.

The Pharisees were stunned to think that any mere man would allow such traitorous, and even blasphemous, behavior. His companion touched him on the arm.

"It's no use, Jotham. You can do nothing. The whole world has gone after him."

The unlikely royal procession continued its descent from the Mount of Olives but stopped at a point just above and overlooking the Golden City—Jerusalem. Dominating the view was the beautiful temple, a dazzling sight as the sun shimmered and danced on its gold encrusted white stone walls. This view had stirred the heart of anyone who beheld it. But Jesus only wept. With tears streaming down his face he lamented the lack of spiritual insight of those within the great stone walls and the sorry end that awaited them because of it.

"If only you knew the things that make for peace, even today it would not be too late. But you have eyes without sight. You cannot see what you need to do. You continue your political intrigues, hoping to overcome your enemies. But in reality the days are coming upon you when your enemies will build an embankment around you, trapping you in the city. Your walls will be dashed to the ground, your people too, because you did not recognize the time when God visited you. The Christ, the Anointed One of God, has come to show you the way of peace, but you will not learn."

In the midst of his triumphant entry into the capital, a weeping Jesus made a terrible prediction. Those about him were stunned, lacking understanding. After all, here was their Savior, their king, right here in their midst. How bad could the future be with their very own king to care for them, to protect them from enemies who would do such terrible things? With hope abounding, future destruction seemed unreal, impossible.

Judas shuddered. What was Jesus saying? That Jerusalem would be destroyed because her inhabitants could not learn the way of peace? But they *were* living in peace, unhappily because it was a forced peace, an uneasy peace that was ensured by the presence of foreign soldiers armed with swords. Judas certainly wanted to live in peace but independent of any tyrant who told them what they must do and punished them relentlessly if they didn't comply.

What indeed had Jesus taught them about? Loving your enemies? Turning the other cheek? Doing good to those who hated you? Impossible! Judas could not fathom such ideas. This was not the way to achieve peace. They needed a rebellion to free Judea of her shackles—then there would be peace. Judas firmly believed it could be had in no other way. Jesus could do it if he would only set his mind to it. And now was the time, judging by the adulation of those all around.

After some minutes the procession tentatively began moving again as the crowd resumed the hosanna refrain. As they came through the gates of the city, the multitude of celebrants seemed to find new energy. The cries of hosanna and the heralding of a great king took on new vigor.

This amazing spectacle took by surprise those in the city who, up to now, were unaware of it. "Who is this man?" could be heard on all sides. The crowd answered, "This is the prophet Jesus from Nazareth of Galilee."

After arriving in Jerusalem, Jesus went directly to the temple and entered the Court of the Gentiles. Here sacrificial animals were sold, animals that had already been pronounced free of blemish by the temple inspectors. Here national monies were also exchanged for temple shekels. The temple provided these services for the benefit of pilgrims, or at least this was the pretense. Since sacrificial victims could be purchased outside for a small fraction of the temple prices, but seldom passed inspection, and since the wealthy Annas controlled the whole system, including the inspectors, there was no question who really benefited.

Jesus stood absorbing the scene before him. There sat fat merchants, arrayed in the finest clothing. Their tunics were of soft linen, girdled with colorful silks. Over this they wore long-sleeved, linen cloaks, the long sleeves being badges of wealth. Worshipers in the market for the necessary victims were being coaxed by highly competitive businessmen. The huckstering on every side overwhelmed the travelers. Consternation at having to pay such high prices flashed across their faces. There seemed to be no room here for the normal bargaining process. The merchants completely controlled the market.

To look at their faces was to see nothing but self-centered indulgence. Eyes, narrow and shrewd, glittered when a sale had been made. Cheeks bulged and jowls hung low, accouterments of self-indulgence. Fat ring-laden fingers extended from greedy hands, recoiling as they came into contact with rough, callous-adorned, work-worn hands in the passing of coins. Honest, hard-working people faced the dilemma of having to forego even some of the necessities of life to buy these exorbitantly priced animals, or not make the required annual sacrifice. This then was a double sacrifice on their part in order that the merchants, and the high priest, could satisfy gluttonous appetites for rich foods and clothe themselves in rich fabrics.

Jesus saw it all. He saw the outward scene, but he also saw within—the self-centeredness on the one hand, the self-denial on the other. The anger welled up within, starting in the pit of his stomach, swelling into his chest, and exploding in terrible rage.

"What do you think you are doing? Don't you know what this building is?"

He strode toward them with anger-hardened eyes, eyes that only a short time earlier had been soft with tears. Storming from one stall to another, he released latches securing lamb pens so that the startled creatures scattered. He upset bird cages, filling the air with gray fury as the pigeons flew in confusion. He overturned tables, scattering coins. Coins rolled away, and kept rolling, losing themselves in corners and chinks.

So completely startled by this uncharacteristic outburst that they could do nothing else, the disciples watched, fascinated, incredulous, immobilized by their own confusion. As the stunned merchants vainly tried to retrieve rolling coins or grab at pigeons in wild flight, Jesus spoke to them in an angry but controlled voice. "It is written, 'My house shall be called a house of prayer,' but you make it a den of robbers."

Men scrambled about the floor, seeking errant coins hiding in cracks and crevices, and muttering such things as, "Where does he get the authority?" and "The high priest will hear of this!" Turning away from the men who had entirely missed the meaning of his words, Jesus started to leave the temple.

As always happened whenever he appeared in public, wherever he turned people were waiting for him, waiting to be healed. He could not leave for the press of the hurting. In a complete reversal of emotion, he moved from anger to compassion, and he did it with no small effort. Those who would respond surrounded him, and they should not suffer his anger. He gently pressed his fingers over the closed eyes of a blind man, thinking, *There are none so blind as those who refuse to see.* That kind of blindness was much more difficult to heal because they did not desire healing. They did not even realize their blindness.

Amidst the revival of interrupted praise, Jesus healed many more people. The blind walked away sighted, as awed as young children who behold something wonderful for the first time. The sick abandoned crutches and discarded their bandages. Those who walked now on strong legs, upright because of straightened backs, rolled up their pallets and tucked them under their arms.

The people came. The people were healed. The people shouted. What a glorious day. Even the unpleasantness in the temple met with the approval of the great crowd of followers, for hadn't those thieves gotten just what they deserved? Finally someone had put them in their place for taking advantage of a religious requirement and a pilgrim's plight. Yes, this man must be their king. He could solve all of their problems.

"Hosanna to the Son of David!" The multitude picked up the chant again. It rang through the temple; it rang through the streets; it rang through the clouds to the heavens. And it pounded into the heads of scowling, skeptical temple prelates. "Do you *hear* what these people are saying?" They flung the question at Jesus.

Again he responded, "Yes, I hear. These are children of the Father. Have you never heard that perfect praise comes from the mouths of babes?" He paused. "Who will silence them? Who *can* silence them?"

Calling the twelve together, he left the temple and made his way to Bethany.

A quiet cluster of men walked the road that evening, each man thinking his own thoughts. What a day! What a day of surprises! Not one of the twelve could have foreseen anything that had happened. If the other disciples were confused, Judas was most confused of all. Jesus entered the great city of Jerusalem as a king. He allowed the people to title him so. But what kind of monarch mingled so freely with the common people, and what kind of a Hebrew king deliberately alienated religious authority?

And what evil could cause these happy people to turn from joyous acclamation to hateful renunciation in less than a week's time?

CHAPTER THREE

Entrapment

Very early in the morning, before the first light of dawn began to paint the sky with delicate pink and lavender tones, before anyone else was stirring, Jesus and the twelve quietly left the house. It was chilly in those early hours before the sun had begun to cast its warmth on the earth, and they all drew their short-sleeved cloaks about them more snugly. They walked along the road to Jerusalem in silence, more tired than awake, first one yawning, then another. One more hour of sleep this morning would have been welcome.

Morning's light soon came, imperceptibly at first. The colors of dawn fingered their way across the sky from behind, finally exploding in glorious celebration as the sun appeared in an ever-growing red ball over the rim of the earth. The whole scene was lost on them as they moved westward from Bethany to Jerusalem, but soon the light overcame the darkness, and the sun's warmth penetrated their backs. Sleep was forgotten. Having had no breakfast, they were more conscious now of hunger.

"I want to return to the temple," Jesus told them. "But first let's get a bit of bread." So they turned off the Bethany Road, taking a southerly direction to come more directly into the Lower City. As they approached the bazaar, its characteristic sounds became evident, even though the hour was early. Merchants enjoyed brisk business in the early hours of the day because people preferred shopping then. It was cooler both in regard to the weather and to tempers, and shoppers enjoyed a better selection too. The hungry men pressed through the crowd until they came to the baker, from whom they purchased several small loaves. Sharing among themselves, they then made their way to the temple, entering through the Royal Porch.

In the meantime the chief priests and scribes who had come together in Solomon's Porch that morning conferred among themselves. Knowing Jesus had returned to Jerusalem and would doubtless come to the temple, they discussed the problem he posed and the threat to their political and religious status. His behavior the day before was outrageous, contemptuous of authority, blasphemous.

These men represented the most venerated and respected group in the land. The chief priests, like all the priests, descended directly from Aaron, brother of Moses and first priest to the Hebrews. They supervised the whole body of priests, which on a daily basis involved one thousand chief priests, priests, and Levites. During festival times, such as Passover, this number swelled to about eighteen thousand. The chief priests also supervised all temple activities and were in charge of both daily and weekly services at the temple. The temple treasury was also their responsibility.

Asa, one of the chief priests, wasted no words but went right to the heart of the problem as he saw it—authority, particularly if it threatened their lucrative source of wealth.

"What authority does this Jesus think he has to interfere with our religious practices? That's what he was doing when he caused such a ruckus here yesterday. None of this is any concern of his. We've sold these animals and changed money in the temple for pilgrims for years. You know as well as I do that it's a necessary service. How else are people who come from great distances to have certified unblemished animals for their sacrifices, or temple shekels for their offerings, if we don't supply them? He's an arrogant upstart."

The others nodded assent. Joram, stroking his beard, muttered, "He has taken upon himself the authority he exercises so readily, and the people accept it without question."

Asa reported Annas' reaction to Jesus' violence of the day before. "Annas was livid when he heard about it. He pounded the table with his fists. His face flushed so red with rage, I thought he would explode." After a pause he added, "Finally he said through clenched teeth, 'There's got to be a way.' Nothing more."

"But that isn't the only problem brought on us yesterday," Tobias reminded them. "Nor is it by any means the most serious one. He has set himself up as our king, the Messiah, if I may dare to say that."

As a scribe Tobias spoke from depths of vast knowledge. The others listened attentively, respectfully, for it was known to all that the scribes possessed great knowledge of the workings of the Lord. A scribe was not even fully ordained until he had studied Scripture and the law for thirty years or more. Whenever a question arose concerning interpretation of the law or of Scripture, a scribe was consulted and heeded.

Joseph, also a scribe, echoed Tobias' concern. "Yes, this business of messiahship is nothing less than blasphemy."

Abijah, a chief priest, countered, "In all fairness, he did not proclaim himself king or Messiah."

"He didn't have to," the angry Joseph retorted. "The people did it for him. But it's all one and the same since he said nothing to stop them. You heard him. He wouldn't even try, saying it was useless. He accepted their praise and adulation as his due."

"In my opinion," Tobias stated, "he has taken upon himself the authority that belongs only to God. He has even been impudent enough in times past to forgive sinners. Only God can do that, everyone knows. Anyone else claiming to be able to do such a thing is nothing but a blasphemer."

Joseph listened as his colleagues discussed the matter. Believing they should do more than just talk about the problem, he said, "We have all spoken with justification. This man Jesus is taking entirely too much upon himself, and he is encouraged by the willingness of the people to believe in him. But talking amongst ourselves doesn't accomplish a thing. We need to act. I suggest we challenge him the next time he comes to the temple. Let's find out where he thinks he has acquired all this authority."

"Yes, of course," Asa agreed. "We must do this."

They all agreed. Tobias was chosen to put the question to Jesus.

It was not long before the opportunity came, for at that moment Jesus and the twelve entered Solomon's Porch. Confident that Jesus would not be able to answer their question without losing his credibility with the people, his inquisitors wasted no time. They walked to meet him in a defiant manner, smug self-satisfaction obvious in their faintly smirking lips. Tobias approached Jesus and asked, "By what authority are you doing these things? Who gave you the authority to heal and to forgive sins?"

Peter winced. *Here it comes now,* he thought. *If Jesus admits that his power and authority have come from God, they will denounce him to the Sanhedrin as a heretic.* Astonished, he listened as Jesus responded without giving them the answer they sought.

"I also will ask you a question; and if you tell me the answer, then I will tell you by what authority I do these things. The baptism of John, did it come from heaven or from men?"

They looked at one another in surprise and consulted among themselves.

"What shall we say now?" Joram asked. "We know that John's baptism was from heaven, because he preached repentance, one of the basic facts of our faith. Only as we repent does God forgive us. This comes directly from God; it is not an idea any man thought up."

"Yes, yes, we know that," Asa impatiently agreed. "But we can't admit that to him, or else he will ask us why we didn't believe in John."

"Then we must say it was from men," Joram suggested.

"Joram, you're not thinking!" Joseph's impatience flung itself at Joram, impatience born of frustration with the whole complicated affair. The position in which they had found themselves was impossible. "If we say it was of men, then the multitude will attack us because they believe John was a prophet."

"Then there is nothing we can say." Joram spoke what they were all thinking.

Tobias turned to Jesus and said, "We do not know." Their pomposity wilted, for they had been ensnared in their own net.

Jesus said to them, "In that case neither will I tell you by what authority I do the things that I do."

Jesus turned to his chosen disciples. "Come around. I want to tell you a story."

The twelve clustered about Jesus, but people passing nearby stopped to listen also. If someone was going to tell a story, they wanted to hear it. Those who knew about Jesus and his stories crowded close, for he was a popular storyteller. He talked about the everyday things in their lives, but everyone went away afterwards with something new to think about. The wonderful thing about it was that his words always made sense. So the crowd pressed in around the disciples. Among them were many Pharisees, not intending to learn but straining instead to catch any hint of heretical theology. Jesus spoke in a conversational manner, his voice strong so that it carried even to the edge of the crowd.

"A householder planted a vineyard. He placed a protective hedge around its borders and equipped it with a winepress and a watchtower. He rented it to tenants and left it in their care while he went to another country. At harvest time he sent some of his servants to gather his grapes. But the tenants took advantage of the situation and mistreated the servants, beating one, stoning another, and killing the third. So the householder sent more servants, and the tenants did the same with them. Finally, believing that they would have more respect for his son, he sent him to gather the fruit of his vineyard. From the watchtower the tenants observed his approach and talked among themselves. 'This is the heir. Let's kill him and then we will have this vineyard for ourselves.' So when he came to them, they grabbed the owner's son, dragged him from the vineyard to the outside of the hedge, and killed him."

Jesus then asked, "When the owner of the vineyard returns, what will he do to his tenants?"

The people murmured among themselves while the Pharisees began conversing together, uncomfortable in the face of truth.

"You know he is talking about Israel," Jotham stated.

"Yes, we understand that only too well," Asher agreed. "We know that the great prophet Isaiah told of a vineyard with a watchtower and a wine vat, fertile and well-cared for, but because it wouldn't produce anything but wild grapes, it was to be destroyed. Isaiah said that vineyard was Israel. Do you think Jesus is trying to tell us that Israel is about to be destroyed? It's preposterous! Isaiah made his prophecy long ago, and nothing has ever happened to us. Jesus is no great prophet, so why should we think he might be right? There is no need to get upset over the words of a man who does not even seem to care about the law and the prophets."

"But he knows the prophets," Jeremias, another Pharisee, spoke up. Intrigued by Jesus and perhaps even tempted to believe in him, he countered Asher's last words. He had listened to Jesus at every opportunity and had been impressed with how well he did know the prophets. "He always quotes from them. Look here, since this story is so similar to that one from our greatest prophet, perhaps Jesus is trying to remind us of it. Maybe it's a warning, and he wants us to understand that it is not too late even now for that prophecy to be fulfilled. We should consider his words."

"No, we should not!" Jotham was irate. "He is a trouble-maker. He tries to stir up the people. If Israel is destroyed, it will be because *he* has influenced the people to ignore the laws of our religion and encourage the ire of Rome by proclaiming our own king—not because we have done anything wrong."

Jotham had no idea how very wrong he was. Perhaps Jeremias was the wiser one.

"But I have observed," Jeremias argued, "that he has not encouraged disobedience of the law and the prophets. He appears to disregard the laws that our own scribes and rabbis have added to the law God gave to Moses in the Ten Commandments."

"Are you too falling under his spell, Jeremias? If you are thinking of becoming a disciple, just remember what happens to heretics—and their sympathizers," Asher warned, waving his finger in front of Jeremias' face. His threatening voice grew weary as he said, "Look now what we have come to. We are divided even among ourselves."

Jotham disagreed. "I think that we are in agreement. Don't worry about Jeremias. He's an impractical dreamer, but he will soon awaken."

"Look, let's not waste time arguing. We haven't even come close to solving our problem," Asher reminded them.

Right he was. Actually, they could not solve the problem, partly because of the division in their own ranks, whether or not

Jotham wished to accept this fact. Some were willing to consider the ideas Jesus taught. There must be something to what he said because he always spoke with such authority. And the people loved him. They believed in him. Were he a fraud, it is doubtful he would have maintained his following for as long as he had. The rest, however, stubbornly refused even to consider any of this. They held to their own ideas about Jesus, which were grounded in the fear of losing status among their own people and of instigating Rome's wrath against their nation. So they argued among themselves.

Having discussed Isaiah's vineyard story and his prophecy, the Pharisees knew the answer but were unwilling to admit it. They turned back to face Jesus, mute in the face of truth.

Jesus had to answer his own question since no one was willing to commit himself to an answer. "He will come and destroy those tenants and give the vineyard to others."

Now *that* they hadn't expected. They were prepared to hear that the vineyard was to be destroyed—but to give it away? Never!

"God forbid!" rang out in a denying chorus of horror. It was unthinkable to any Pharisee who understood the significance of Jesus' words that the kingdom would be taken from Israel, the chosen people of God. That could only mean it would be given to Gentiles.

The idea of the kingdom of God was not new to these Jewish listeners. The chief priests and Pharisees understood very well the reality of God's kingdom for they believed themselves to be in it. The people of Israel knew God as their King. The Pharisees believed, and the scribes too, that it was their responsibility to see that all the people obeyed the laws of God. Only as long as they remained obedient to those laws would God be King over Israel. What would become of them if God no longer kept his vineyard, his nation Israel? Life without God over it all would be empty life. To lose everything because of a lack of vigilance would be the worst of circumstances. Yes, they must remain strict, make sure all of God's laws were kept.

The Pharisees originated in the days of the Hasmoneans. During that time the king was also the high priest. This had troubled some of the Jewish thinkers of the day because it violated a part of their law. A group had formed that was dedicated to the keeping of the law. These Pharisees existed to make sure that all Jews strictly kept the law. But the present-day Pharisees found that they had to oversee a rebellious and ignorant lot, or at least that was how they saw it. Jesus made their formidable task even more difficult. Something was going to have to be done about him—and soon.

Jesus explained his statement. "Have you never read in the Scripture, 'The very stone which the builders rejected has become the head of the corner; this was the Lord's doing, and it is marvelous in our eyes?' That's what I have told you in this story. This nation has betrayed the Father so the kingdom of God will be taken away from it and given to another nation that will produce the fruit of it."

Anger welled up within the chief priests and Pharisees. How could Jesus presume to say such a thing? No other nation on earth was worthy to be God's kingdom. The Gentile nations were pagan. Having never recognized God as the one God, they were not deserving of such an honor. No other nation had God's promise of a partnership with him. God had promised this honor to the nation of Israel back in Abraham's time with the words, "I will be your God and you will be my people," and that promise had been renewed with Moses. Angered at the audacity of Jesus to challenge God's covenant, Joseph and Asa rushed to seize him but were kept from him by the people.

"No, you cannot touch him!"

"He is a prophet. Leave him alone!"

Jesus' angered followers pushed the two men away. They hurriedly left the crowd and met together in the home of Joram to take counsel.

"That was a risky and foolhardy thing we tried to do," Joseph sputtered. "We must think this thing out more carefully. We cannot be so clumsy."

"You are right, of course. We could have been killed." Asa still trembled from the fright he sustained. "We might have been killed!" he repeated. "They really believe he is a great prophet."

"I suggest," Joseph said, having calmed down somewhat, "that the only thing to do now is to wait. We must look for the right opportunity, when there are not enough people around to protect him."

"I agree that caution must be observed," Tobias said. "But how long can we wait?" He scratched his head absent-mindedly, trying to solve the puzzle. "It seems to me that the longer we take to act, the more time he has to increase his following."

"But what else can we do?" Asa asked, still agitated. "You saw what happened out there, right on the very steps of the temple."

The group became quiet, pondering the dilemma. Then Tobias spoke again. "You know how the people cling to every word he utters. So why not trap him by his own words? If all those loyal followers heard him say something they didn't like, they would fall away soon enough."

"That's it," Joseph agreed. "We must have a question that will incriminate him no matter what answer he gives. And we must send someone to pose the question who won't be known to anyone there."

So the Pharisees sent out some of their own disciples as spies. They formulated a question that mattered greatly to the people, which gave them great pleasure as they contemplated the outcome. The Pharisees knew that if Jesus answered one way, it would incite the anger of the crowd against him as a Roman sympathizer. If he answered the opposite way, he would encourage the people to break Roman law, exposing himself to the danger of defying Rome, and Rome would dispose of him for them. They felt smugly proud of themselves at being so clever.

The spies worked their way through the crowd until they stood directly in front of Jesus. Tirzah spoke out, "Teacher, we know that you are true, and teach the way of God truthfully, and care for no man; for you do not regard the position of men. Tell us, then, what do you think? Is it lawful to pay taxes to Caesar or not?"

The prefacing sentence had not deceived Jesus. Neither was he ignorant of this man or his mission. He stood considering him for several moments, until Tirzah became very uncomfortable, sensing that his mission already had been lost.

Jesus looked straight into his eyes and said to him, "Why do you have to put me to the test, you hypocrites?"

He turned to Judas. "Show me the money for the tax."

Judas handed him the coin, and Jesus asked, "Whose likeness and inscription is on this coin?"

"Caesar's!" someone called out.

Jesus said to them, "Whatever belongs to Caesar, give it to him, and give to God the things that are God's."

Having received their unexpected answer, the disciples of the Pharisees left, amazed at the ability of this man to walk into traps yet remain unsnared. They also departed in some trepidation about what their teachers would say of their failed mission.

When the Pharisees' disciples had left, Jesus continued teaching, speaking to those who were interested in learning something from him. Though Jesus enjoyed this respite, it would prove to be short-lived.

Word of the thwarted debates attempted by the scribes and the Pharisees had reached some of the Sadducees. The Sadducees and the Pharisees were not friendly toward each other. They often opposed each other in scriptural interpretation and had taken opposite positions in matters relating to the Roman occupation. Whereas the Pharisees refused to take an oath of allegiance to the Romans, the Sadducees accepted Roman authority and espoused the Roman culture. They were the elite of the Jews and, as the controlling figures in the Sanhedrin, possessed great political power. They believed that through their cooperation with Rome, they could continue to maintain this power and also keep Palestine safe from any action against them. Because of their alliance with the Romans, they were not respected by the common people and therefore had less influence over them than the Pharisees. The high priests, Annas and Caiaphas, belonged to this group, as did the lower priests.

Jesus threatened the Sadducees' precarious position and power. So when they heard of the Pharisees' loss, they decided they had better attempt to silence this man. At least in the matter of Jesus the two groups agreed.

Enan sat drumming his fingers on the table as he listened to Reuben.

"I tell you, Enan," Reuben said, "things have come to a critical point. The people are so enamored with this man, they could easily do something foolish. Strictly speaking, they already have by proclaiming him king, but so far nothing seems to have come of that. Wherever he goes, throngs eagerly anticipate every word he utters. As his popularity continues to grow, so will the demand that he accept David's throne. And what do you think is going to happen when Roman authorities hear that we have got ourselves a king, our own king? Do you think Tiberius will sit still for that? Not for a minute! We'll have more trouble on our hands than any of us ever thought possible."

Enan nodded but said nothing. Reuben fell silent, sensing that Enan was deep in thought.

After some minutes had passed Reuben continued, "You know, Enan, if Rome has to quell an uprising, it will be ugly and violent. They don't waste any sympathy on troublemakers. And if that happens, the practice of our religion will be forbidden. Where will that leave us? The Sanhedrin will be disbanded. We will be out. There will be no more reason for us to exist. Indeed, I do not think it is far-fetched to suppose that we could expect worse from the Romans than the reprehensible acts of Antiochus IV."

Enan shuddered at Reuben's last words. "God forbid that it should ever happen again!" he burst out.

"No, it must not," quietly agreed Reuben. "Not another persecution. That is what makes this matter so important."

It was hard to imagine that there could ever again exist such a monster as Antiochus, would-be exterminator of the Jews, desecrator of the temple, would-be destroyer of the religion that worshiped the one true God. He would have succeeded in destroying Judaism if God had not interceded on their behalf. God provided them with brave men. Mattathias and his five sons, especially Judas, saved them in the end from the savage enemy.

At that moment another of their members, ushered by a servant, entered the room. Ahira glanced at Enan, who had now begun to pace the room, then turned to Reuben and said, "You've been discussing the matter of Jesus?"

"Yes," Reuben replied. "I think we must try to do something. The Pharisees have had no success."

"I've been thinking about it," Ahira said. "Jesus claims to have raised people from the dead, or at least that's what we hear from his followers. Since we don't believe in resurrection, even though the Pharisees do, perhaps we could question him on that point. It would be a good way to entangle him as he tries to explain something about which our two bodies have always been in opposition."

"That's a good idea." The agitated Enan had stopped pacing. "Now let's see, how can we put the question?"

The three worked together, wording the question that Reuben would ask Jesus. It must be just right, leaving no cracks through which the clever Jesus could slip, thereby denying them success.

So these men came to Jesus toward the middle of the afternoon. Reuben approached him and presented him with the problem.

"Teacher, Moses said, 'If a man dies, having no children, his brother must marry the widow and raise children for his brother.' Once there were seven brothers among us; the oldest one married and died soon thereafter, leaving no children. The second brother, and the third, and down to the seventh brother all married this woman, and all died, leaving no children. Finally the woman died. Our question is, 'Whose wife will she be in the resurrection since in this life she was wife to all of them?'"

Again Jesus contemplated his questioners in silence for several moments before answering. "You are wrong because you do not know Scripture, and you do not know the power of God. In the resurrection no one marries; they are like angels in heaven. As for the resurrection of the dead, haven't you read the Scripture? You speak of Moses. At the burning bush when God spoke to him, he said, 'I am the God of Abraham, and the God of Isaac, and the God of Jacob.' God is not the God of the dead but the God of the living."

Left speechless, Reuben faded wordlessly back into the crowd. Leaning toward Ahira, he whispered, "What could I say? How does he always manage to have the last word?"

Joab, a scribe who had been silent in clandestine gatherings of scribes and Pharisees earlier in the day, spoke up. "Teacher, you have spoken well."

After that the Sadducees did not dare to ask him any more questions. Jesus was too quick for them, and his answers made *them* look foolish.

The Pharisees remained hopeful, however. Seeing that Jesus had silenced the Sadducees, they decided on another question to test him. Jotham strode forward and said to Jesus, "Teacher, which is the great commandment in the Law?"

"You shall love the Lord your God with all your heart, and with all your soul, and with all your mind. This is the great and first commandment. And a second is like it. You shall love your neighbor as yourself. On these two commandments depend all the law and the prophets. There are no commandments greater than these."

Again Joab the scribe was impressed. "You are right, Teacher. You have truly said that he is one, and there is no other but he; and to love him with all the heart, and with all the understanding, and with all the strength, and to love one's neighbor as oneself, is much more than all whole burnt offerings and sacrifices." Here was one who, in his many years of scribal training and reading of the prophets, had found the taproot of the whole body of Scripture—that God is love, and that this love is far more important in God's eyes than legalistic rituals that deny justice.

When Jesus heard the wise and perceptive response of this man, he spoke softly, his eyes glistening, "You are not far from the kingdom of God."

Now even the Pharisees fell silent. It seemed they could say nothing to cause Jesus to make the slightest theological error—or even a political one. They were finished. And with each confrontation it seemed that one more of the religious elite became known to them as a secret disciple. Their position was weakening.

The people heard Jesus and were comforted, knowing that here at last was a leader who would loosen the bonds of rigid law. As he responded to each baited question, they found it exciting. Some nodded assent; some were more vocal. But however they responded, they felt united in their acceptance of this man who understood the real meaning of life. He knew that the Pharisees with all their devotion to law and tradition, the Sadducees with all their power and prestige, the scribes with all their learning, and the priests with all their ceremony knew nothing except how to find fault with everyone who did not comply with their rigid standards. Yes, to love one's neighbor honored God more than all the sacrifices one could make in a lifetime. And loving one's neighbor meant to love God. It was as simple as that.

Then Jesus asked a question of the Pharisees who still stood about. "What do you think of the Christ? Whose son is he?"

"Why, he is the son of David."

"How is it then that David, inspired by the Spirit, calls him Lord, saying, 'The Lord said to my Lord, Sit at my right hand till I put thy enemies under thy feet?' If David thus calls the Christ, the anointed one, Lord, how can he be his son? How can God's anointed king, who has not yet come, be the son of David?"

The scribes had always taught that the Messiah would be the son of David, his descendant, therefore the conquering King of the Jews. Jesus tried to tell them that the Messiah was David's Lord, the Son of God. Caught off guard by Jesus' rationale, the scribes had no answer. For once there was no ready authoritative response on their lips.

After waiting a few minutes for the answer that was not to come, and in the hearing of all the people, Jesus said, "Beware of the scribes, who love to go about in long robes, and to have salutations in the marketplaces and the best seats in the synagogues and the places of honor at feasts, who devour widow's houses and for a pretense make long prayers. They will receive the greater condemnation. With all of their long years of study and training they should know better."

Having risen to a position of great importance, the scribes believed themselves to have the power of judgment over the people they were supposed to be guiding. They interpreted the laws of God, but in an attempt to be exact in their interpretation, they had become encumbered in a large body of tradition, of which most of the finer points were lost on the ordinary person. In their zeal to ensure obedience to all aspects of their law and tradition, they had lost sight of human need. The very people whom they wanted to bring closer to God through obedience to his laws, they had instead shut out of the kingdom, as they understood it. Those whom they regarded as sinners, anyone who broke any of the laws regardless of how trivial—but particularly tax collectors and harlots—were banned from the temple.

Jesus ruthlessly condemned the scribes for this reason. He hated laws and traditions that kept people outside the sphere of God's kingdom, and he had no time for such blatant disregard for the real intent of God's law as embodied in the Great Commandment.

So Jesus, in a burst of anger born of long-held impatience at such self-righteous attempts at judgment, lashed out at the mighty scribes in a scathing diatribe.

Never had his listeners heard such things said about their leaders. It was not prudent to complain about or find fault with the religious leaders, though in private many complained. As shocked as they may have been, however, they were pleased and relieved to learn that they did not have to regard the scribes as powerful guards of their destiny. The traditional laws numbered in the thousands, and who could know them well enough never to break any? It was a heavy burden, and Jesus had just released them from it.

As far as Jesus was concerned, it was much more important that each person treat others out of love and respect and understanding. Hadn't he once told them, "Whatever you wish that men would do to you, do so to them?" This statement summed up the law and the prophets. Here was a simple law, easy to understand yet profound in its consequences.

Retreating from the crowd, Jesus sat down on a marble bench in the Court of the Women. His face was drawn; dark shadows were evident under his eyes. Wearied from the long day of confrontation with antagonistic religious chauvinists, he needed breathing space. Gathering the twelve about him, creating an island of solitude in the midst of throngs, he allowed his body and mind to relax.

He watched the people as they came to give alms. The bright reds and blues, the golds, and the greens of the wealthy stood out prominently among the earth colors of the common people. The sheen of silks contrasted sharply with the rough texture of homespun fabrics. Considerable, noisy fanfare accompanied that brilliant display of color. It seemed that every wealthy person from miles around had come, each with his own trumpeter, in effect announcing, "Here I am. Notice the large sum I am putting into the treasury box. Be impressed with my generosity." Following the trumpeter walked a servant bearing the extravagant offering while a beaming, self-satisfied, and expensively dressed contributor basked in the awe and admiration of his own imagination.

It never occurred to him that the less fortunate around him didn't praise him at all for his generosity. Instead they remembered his thumb on the scale as only yesterday one of them had purchased cheese or received a short weight of grain. No, it was not admiration. If these less fortunate people paid any attention at all, it was more likely with disdain than awed admiration.

Jesus noticed all of this. As he watched the people deposit their offerings in the box, a tiny woman, very old and obviously very poor, crept up to the treasury box, trying her best to be invisible. She quickly dropped in two small coins, two copper coins that together amounted to only one penny. Having done this, she quickly crept away. Calling the disciples' attention to her, Jesus said, "Truly, I say to you, this poor widow has put in more than all of them. They gave out of their abundance, but she, in her poverty, gave everything she had, her whole living."

Was there sadness in his tone?

June 23, 2008

Dear Fran,

Please accept my apologies for this oversight. I don't know how I let that get by me. I remember you were the first to be willing to wait.

What makes it really hard for me to understand my forgetting is that, even after returning home, I had been thinking about what I wanted to say in your book.

I dated it as May since that was when I was there. I hope that's all right.

Again, my sincerest apologies to a most gracious lady.

Fondly,

Elizabeth

When Jesus rose to go, the disciples were ready. It had been a very long day, and this final episode seemed insignificant, though admittedly touching, compared to all that had happened. Yet was it really? Some indefinable thread connected the self-centeredness of the wealthy and the selflessness of the poor widow to the day's events. The truth is that Jesus had just given them a message that was related to all he had taught them about God's kingdom. Perhaps one day they would be able to make the connection.

The immense walls of the temple enclosure dwarfed them as they left through a western gate. Looking at the massive stone slabs towering above them, they were impressed by their sturdiness and seeming permanence. One of them, Simon, called Jesus' attention to the sight that awed them so.

"Look, Teacher, what wonderful stones and what wonderful buildings."

What Simon looked at was a most amazing sight—the one bright jewel in the tarnished crown of Herod the Great. Here was a building designed and engineered by the finest craftsmen of Phoenicia. Only the purest white marble had been used in construction and the finest quality limestone. Plates of fine gold, the best available, adorned large areas of the walls. Carpenters had used wood from the great cedars of Lebanon.

But Jesus was unimpressed. "You see all these, do you not? There is coming a day when there will not be left here one stone upon another, that will not be thrown down."

Judas scoffed inwardly. Everyone knew this temple would last hundreds of years, maybe thousands. Herod had built it well. The very wall they looked at was built of such huge stones that it staggered the imagination to think how men could have lifted them into place. The masonry was so well done that each stone fitted perfectly into the adjacent one. It would be virtually impossible to destroy such walls. *What a strange man I've joined myself to, and he's becoming more strange every day, every moment.*

The eclipse of Judas' personality advanced rapidly. The dark thoughts that had begun some months ago, and had been given room to grow, now took command. Judas had allowed himself to be taken prisoner by a relentless jailer. Satan's key at last controlled the lock to Judas' heart.

Again Jesus led the disciples to Bethany, away from the agitation that Jerusalem now signified. Bethany meant the companionship of loving friends, a relaxing meal, respite from clamor, confusion, condemnation.

But if Jesus was resting, others were not. The Pharisees, the scribes, the priests, and the Sadducees took every available moment to confer, planning how to silence this man who had become so dangerous to them. This outspoken man endangered all that they knew and stood for. He questioned their religious laws and practices. Even their nation faced the danger of destruction. Rome would show them no clemency if the Emperor Tiberius had reason to believe an insurrection was fomenting.

These rulers debated vigorously about how to solve the dilemma, but no one could agree what to do because they all feared the people. Many among these religious elite had believed in Jesus, but they were silent. They feared if they confessed such belief, they would be put out of the temple. They valued what their colleagues thought of them over obedience to the truth they had discovered in Jesus. So no one spoke up for Jesus. The only thing in his favor was the lack of agreement among his enemies.

Caiaphas, the high priest, succinctly stated the purpose of their plotting, as he tried to focus their minds on a common thought. "It is expedient that one man die for the people." If the one man, Jesus, did not die, then many would die. Little did he know that, flawed though he was, he had just prophesied for God.

Joram confirmed the statement. "You are absolutely right. Obviously our difficulty is in not knowing how to go about it, but we must give all of our time and attention to this matter until it is accomplished."

CHAPTER FOUR

Parables

It had been a restless night for most of the thirteen that again trekked the road from Bethany to Jerusalem. Jesus had been uncharacteristically blunt and outspoken in the past couple days. The disciples had some difficulty coping with their shock at his behavior. It seemed so dissonant with the loving, forgiving nature of the Jesus they had come to know. What he said was necessary; *how* he said it was incomprehensible to them. Tension filled the air everywhere they went; it even followed them to Bethany.

So much had happened to change their normal routine that it was hard to know anymore what to expect. No longer were the days peaceful and exhilarating as they had been when day had followed day, one upon another in much the same manner. They used to walk from one place to another and watch with pride as Jesus told stories or healed the sick. The way he could heal not only the body, but mind and spirit as well, inspired them.

When Jesus let them participate in his ministry, they were filled with trepidation. They had not felt ready yet to go out on their own. But he had sent them out anyway, to teach and to heal, and their success awed them.

Over the past three years they had been surrounded by adoring crowds who couldn't get close enough to Jesus. They clamored for more and more of his time. The people loved Jesus, as he loved them. Whatever was happening, they had always felt at peace with themselves and their world. When masses of people surrounded Jesus, as was usually the case, it was not peaceful or quiet, yet the disciples had no feelings of fear. The peace they felt came from the sense of knowing that all was right.

When the work became too exhausting, they simply retired to a quiet place where they could recoup some measure of tranquility. This would refresh them to be able to minister once again. They had come to cherish those retreat times because they had Jesus to themselves, just teacher and students apart from the rest of the world. During these times Jesus patiently helped them understand what he was teaching.

Now, however, their predictable world had changed; they could no longer anticipate a day's events. This radical alteration of their daily lives unnerved them so that, even after a night's respite in Bethany, it seemed to them no more peace was to be found. Fear became a constant companion.

Having come again to the temple, they went into the courtyard. In a matter of moments people had gathered around, anxious to be near the beloved teacher-healer.

Jesus turned to the Pharisees standing nearby and asked a riddle.

"What do you think? A man had two sons. He went to the first and said, 'Son, go and work in the vineyard today.' But the son said, 'I will not go,' but later he was sorry for what he had said to his father and he went. Then the father went to the second son and told him the same thing. His response was, "I go, sir,' but he did not go. Which of the two sons did his father's will?"

"The first."

"And I say to you, the tax collectors and harlots go into the kingdom of God before you. John came to you preaching the way of righteousness, but you would not listen. You refused to believe, but they listened and believed, and even when you saw the way of righteousness clearly before you, you still would not repent and believe him."

The people standing about were delighted. "Yes, we believed John, and we believe you. To do what is right is better than promises."

Jesus smiled at such simplicity. *Yes*, he thought, *only with childlike understanding can one really accept the truth of the Father.* Complicated laws and big theological words do not change lives.

The Pharisees were not so happy. "Tax collectors and harlots in the kingdom of God? Incredible! We do not even allow such sinners in the temple!"

A Pharisee called Jacob, thin-lipped and narrow-eyed, spoke in a high-pitched voice. He could not imagine a worse prospect. "What good are all of our strict laws if those who break them can enter the kingdom anyway?"

Though he was reticent to speak in the august company of these inflexible colleagues, who tenaciously clung to their traditions and were never willing to give credence to new ideas, Jeremias spoke timidly.

"But Jesus, as did John the prophet before him, leaves room for repentance. It's obvious that Jesus believes that anyone can be forgiven of even the worst sin if he recognizes that he needs forgiveness and asks God for that forgiveness. One who truly repents will no longer want to sin against God, and by so doing, will have attained righteousness. Why then shouldn't such people be allowed into the kingdom? And in the temple too, for that matter." He spoke the last phrase under his breath, but those next to him did not miss it.

"You speak like a fool, Jeremias," Jacob spat at him. "The kingdom and the temple are for those who have been perfect. If sinners were permitted in the kingdom, its perfection would be defiled by their sin. That's why we have developed our laws so thoroughly. They are stated, and all possible ramifications are explained, so that people know exactly what is expected of them. There can be no excuses for disobedience."

With some effort, and exhibiting uncharacteristic courage, Jeremias countered, "But that's just the point. There are so many laws, and so many laws within laws, that except for those of us who have spent years studying, it is impossible to know all of them. Infractions are inevitable and often unknowing. None of that matters, though, if what Jesus says is true. Only that individuals know they are sinners and want to repent is important. Once done, they are doing the Father's will, just as the son who repented of his rudeness to his father.

"The trouble with a lot of us is that we think we have been so righteous that we have no need for repentance. That is why those whom we consider terrible sinners will be in the kingdom before us. They know they have sinned and will have asked God for forgiveness and will be considered righteous. I'm not sure about some of us who are cursed by an inflexible self-righteousness that leaves no room for repentance."

Jeremias' voice shook as he concluded the longest speech he had ever made. He had risked a lot by what he said, especially his last sentence. The other Pharisees regarded him with astonishment, some clicking their tongues in disapproval.

Jesus prevented further discussion. "Let me tell you another parable."

"The kingdom of heaven may be compared to a king who gave a marriage feast for his son. The invited guests refused to come. Even when the king again sent servants to tell them, 'My dinner is ready, my oxen and my fat calves are killed, and everything is prepared. Come to the marriage feast,' they would not come but made light of it. Some made excuses about needing to attend to business or visit their farm, while the rest seized his servants, treated them shamefully, and killed them.

"Finally he said to his servants, 'The wedding is ready, but those invited were not worthy. Go out into the highways and byways, and invite to the marriage feast as many as you find.' So the servants went out into the streets and brought back all whom they found, both bad and good, so that the wedding hall was filled with guests. But when the king came in to look at the guests, he saw there a man who had no wedding garment, and he said to him, 'Friend, how did you get in here without a wedding garment?' The man was speechless. Then the king said to the attendants, 'Bind him and throw him out.' For many are called but few are chosen."

This parable astounded the Pharisees more than ever. "Who would be so foolish as to ignore the king's invitation?" questioned Jotham. This mystery puzzled them. To be an invited guest at the marriage feast of the king's son bestowed the highest honor. To refuse it showed the ultimate disrespect.

"It is possible that other important matters could arise, making it impossible to spend so many days idling about at a wedding feast," conceded Asher. "Such things do happen. What bothers me is the king's willingness to socialize with the undesirables. After all, what have shiftless beggars done to deserve such honorable treatment?"

"I think you miss the point. What business could be more important than sharing in the joy of a wedding feast in the house of the king? The point of the story is that those invited guests made up invalid excuses simply because they didn't want to be bothered going. Rightfully so the king was angry." Jeremias had become emboldened by his newfound ability to speak out. "As the story indicates, the king does not have to concern himself with those who are disinterested and rude. There are plenty of others who long for the good life, and when the king calls, they are ready and eager to accept the invitation. The king wants to celebrate; a celebration needs joyful people—people who are happy and honored to be present."

"But the duties of conducting a business are important, and sometimes unexpected problems arise. Even the king would recognize this," Asher persisted.

"Doesn't a good businessman prepare himself to be able to keep his commitments? Jesus indicated that the king sent the invitations out early enough that the guests would have plenty of time to plan ahead. And as you well know, those who were invited would have already accepted long before the time of the feast. The truth is that the invited guests simply did not care. They were too busy with their routines, their own small social circles. Jesus seems to say that the only people who are excluded from the kingdom are those who exclude themselves."

"What of the man not dressed suitably?" countered Asher. "He was willing to be there, but he was excluded."

"Obviously he didn't care either. Since the king would have had wedding clothes provided, and he didn't accept them, this could only mean he didn't really want to be an acceptable guest, pleasing to the king. He still kept himself apart from the others by his choice. Perhaps Jesus meant that the kingdom does not include all so-called undesirables but only those who truly want to belong and have prepared themselves by repenting, that is, by putting on the wedding clothes."

Again Jesus halted the discussion. "I want to tell you one more parable.

"Once when a man was going on a journey, he called three of his servants and divided his property among them. He gave to one five talents, to another two, and to the third he gave one, each according to his ability. Then he went away. The ones who had received the five and the two talents invested the money and doubled it. The one who had received only one talent hid the money, burying it in the ground.

"After a long absence the master of those servants came and settled accounts with them. The one who had received the five talents came forward, bringing ten talents and saying, 'Master, you delivered to me five talents. Here I have made five talents more.' His master said to him, 'Well done, good and faithful servant. You have been faithful over a little, I will set you over much. Enter into the joy of your master.' Also the one who had two talents presented the master with four and received the same commendation.

"When the third one, who had received the one talent, came forward and presented the master with only his original investment, he said, 'Master, I knew you to be a hard man, reaping where you did not sow, and gathering where you did not winnow, so I was afraid. I went and hid your talent in the ground. Here you have what is yours.'

"But the master answered him, 'You wicked and slothful servant! You knew that I reap where I have not sowed and gather where I have not winnowed? Then you ought to have invested my money with the bankers, and at my coming I should have received what was my own with interest. So take the talent from him, and give it to him who has the ten talents. For to every one who has will more be given, and he will have abundance, but from him who has not, even what he has will be taken away. And cast the worthless servant into the outer darkness.'"

"What a harsh sentence for a man who was merely trying to be prudent," Asher commented.

"It would seem so at first," Joram responded. "But after all, he was a businessman. Unless an investment turned a profit, it was of no use to him."

"What does this have to do with us?" Asher asked.

"Perhaps Jesus wants us to understand that it isn't important what we have, but what we do with what we have," suggested the scribe, Joab. "And if we don't use what we have, no matter how insignificant it seems to us, then we might as well not have it. In fact, we lose it. The master gave the one talent to the man who had ten because he knew it would be used well, not just buried away doing no one any good."

Jesus continued with another story.

"When the Son of man comes in his glory, and all the angels with him, then he will sit on his glorious throne. Before him will be gathered all the nations, and he will separate them one from another as a shepherd separates the sheep from the goats, and he will place the sheep at his right hand, but the goats at the left.

"Then the king will say to those at his right hand, 'Come, O blessed of my Father, inherit the kingdom prepared for you from the foundation of the world. For I was hungry and you gave me food; I was thirsty and you gave me drink; I was a stranger and you welcomed me; I was naked and you clothed me; I was sick and you came to me.'

"Then the righteous will answer him, 'Lord, when did we see you hungry and feed you, or thirsty and give you drink? And when did we see you a stranger and welcome you, or naked and clothe you? And when did we see you sick or in prison and visit you?'

"And the king will answer them, 'I say this to you in truth, as you did it to one of the least of these my brethren, you did it to me.' Then he will say to those at his left hand, 'Depart from me, you cursed, into the eternal fire prepared for the devil and his angels. For I was hungry and you gave me no food; I was thirsty and you gave me no drink; I was a stranger and you did not welcome me; naked and you did not clothe me, sick and in prison and you did not visit me.' Then he will answer them, 'Truly, I say to you, as you did it not to one of the least of these, you did it not to me.' And they will go away into eternal punishment but the righteous into eternal life."

Concluding his sayings, Jesus left the temple.

The compounded parable provided a thought-provoking sermon to serious-minded listeners. Among them sat Lazarus, who had taken advantage of every opportunity to hear Jesus each day. He turned to the man next to him and commented, in an attempt to engage him in discussion, "The Master had powerful thing to say today, my friend."

"That he did, and doesn't he always?"

As the crowd dispersed, they talked as they walked.

"The kingdom he speaks of, don't you think this is in the future as well as now?" Lazarus wanted very much to hear what another might think about his beloved Jesus and his teachings. "It sounds like a kingdom that will last forever, one that has its beginnings here and now for anyone who is willing to accept God as sovereign."

"He has spoken of the kingdom often these two days," the man called Jude added. "And he makes it very clear that all are welcome. It would seem that if we are not included, it's by our own choice. Our great leaders were very disturbed that Jesus intimated yesterday that our nation might no longer be keeper of the kingdom but that some other nation would. They were equally adamant that sinners should not be a part of this kingdom. But the way I see it, this is so much better. It means God is not exclusive like the Pharisees. It means God wants in his kingdom anyone who wants to be there and is willing to repent of past wrongs and be governed by him whether Jew or Gentile, sinful or religious, rich or poor."

Lazarus stopped in his tracks, impulsively grasping Jude by both shoulders. "Yes, yes, you are right." His eyes glistening, his face alight, he enthusiastically endorsed the man's comments. "A kingdom where all are welcome; all are equal. Yes, that would be the very thing Jesus would want. He has never allowed what a person was to keep him from treating that person in a loving, caring manner."

Lazarus' impulsive behavior and hearty response surprised Jude, but as he talked on Jude also sensed the deep and wonderful meaning of what he had just said. He took Lazarus by the shoulder and out of sheer joy they embraced one another as brothers, though before this day they had never met.

When they had resumed walking, Jude asked Lazarus, "What did you make of this morning's discourse?"

Lazarus responded carefully, thinking his way through. "It seems to me he said three things—well, four, if you consider the first parable about the two sons. The most important thing was that repentance is necessary to enter the kingdom. But preparedness is essential and so is faithfulness. And in that last story about the sheep and the goats, I think he said we must be willing to be servants, and this would show God that our love for him was genuine."

"Yes, that does make sense," Jude agreed. "And in the parable about the talents, I believe he said that whatever gifts we have, we must use, or else we will lose them. He wasn't really focused on money, I don't think. He meant our God-given abilities. God's gifts are meant to be used in the best way we know how, and to be used for his purposes, and should never be put aside. But why do you suppose in the last parable the 'sheep' and the 'goats' were surprised about what they had or had not done?"

"You mean, if I were kind enough to offer a thirsty man a cup of water, I would know I had served God?" Lazarus asked.

"Yes, but the 'sheep' didn't seem to be aware of that," observed Jude.

"True," Lazarus agreed. "Perhaps it's because we do not see God's face in those whom we serve. It's an unusual idea. Jesus has given me something new to think about."

"And to me also," Jude said.

After they had walked along in silence for a time, reflecting on this thought, Lazarus spoke aloud his thoughts. "It could be that it goes deeper than that. Perhaps it's that the ways we serve one another come from something within that causes us to care, and so we just do what needs to be done, without thinking about it. Then we are surprised at the commendation that might come because our deed had seemed so natural. This is a different thing than doing good for the sake of a reward. Service that is natural and not seeking reward is the only true service, don't you think?"

Jude nodded agreement. "And such people will live forever in the kingdom. Jesus said that to serve in love means life. Whoever ignores the needs of others, those who are so ensnared in their own self-centeredness that they do not even see others' needs, will never see the coming kingdom. By their own blindness they will not be able to see the door."

The men walked on deep in thought until they parted company, Lazarus turning toward Bethany, Jude toward Ramah. They bade each other farewell with the expressed hope that they might meet again.

As Jude and Lazarus took their separate ways, Jesus and the twelve found it difficult to get away from the temple area. As usual the demand for Jesus' healing abilities came from every side, postponing his desired departure for Bethany. The past three days had been more taxing than usual, and he was anxious for respite. Jesus had been teaching, preaching, healing—that was usual. Now he had been sapped of energy by intense emotions, such as anger and anxiety, and the knowledge that time was closing in on him. So much was still left to be said.

Ready to go back to Bethany, Jesus looked forward to relaxing among his friends who would demand nothing of him. Tomorrow he would not return to the restless city until it was time to gather for the Passover meal he had arranged. He could feel the vibrations within the walls of Jerusalem, just as his disciples had, and sensed an undertone of discontent. He knew that religious officials intended to destroy him. They were merely biding their time, hoping for a favorable moment in the near future.

Jesus had other reasons, however, for avoiding the city on the morrow. If the past three days had been physically and emotionally demanding, he knew they could not compare with what would be required of him in ensuing days. Throughout the three years of his ministry, he had kept up with the daily demands on him only by allowing himself rest periods in which to strengthen his spiritual lifeline to the Father. If ever he needed strengthening of body and spirit, it was now, and he would use the coming day for that purpose. So they parted the crowds at last and descended the steps to the road.

Once on the Bethany road Jesus turned to his disciples, the faithful men who had stayed with him, who had willingly been taught by him, who loved him, and said, "You know that after two days the Passover is coming, and the Son of man will be delivered up to be crucified." He stated it bluntly—a fact to be recognized, dealt with, but not questioned.

Shocked, the men momentarily fell speechless.

Judas didn't know what to think. Since deciding to offer his help to the Council regarding Jesus, his state of confusion had intensified. He had been encouraged by the events on the first day of the week when Jesus had entered Jerusalem as a king and when the people had acclaimed him. Jesus' irrational behavior at the temple and his foolish words about its destruction had just as quickly discouraged him. At times his determination to act had been strengthened, but still he had allowed two full days to pass without making any effort to contact the Council. As much as he felt was wrong about Jesus, he could not help but remember other days when he felt so much was right about Jesus, and how much he had once loved him.

The fact was, however, that Jesus was not living up to Judas' expectations. He had wanted him to be king of the Jews. Instead Jesus claimed to be the long-awaited Messiah, the Holy One, the Son of God. This was blasphemy, and the penalty for blasphemy was death. He had all the evidence he needed but still had not approached the Council, and he didn't really know why.

Jesus had just predicted his own death, and very soon. The prospect of it frightened Judas. But he hadn't done anything yet, only thought about it. Could Jesus have known his thoughts? Could he have heard something today to give him this idea? Only two days away, he had said.

He must have heard something, Judas thought. *Something I didn't hear. Somehow he's heard of a plot. But how? We were never far from each other.* This prediction truly puzzled Judas.

Peter struggled with his own questions. He could not confront Jesus about his prediction of imminent death, as he wanted. He had done so once before and had been severely reprimanded. But he could not keep his thoughts to himself. He grabbed Simon by the shoulder to detain him, and the two fell back from the others.

"Why does he say such things? Now he even tells us when it should be and that the time is close at hand. I cannot accept such talk. It is impossible to imagine."

Simon looked at Peter quizzically. "Impossible to imagine? You can say that after these past three days? He knew he angered the temple officials, yet he continued to speak his mind. It isn't too hard to see the possibility."

"You sound almost cold hearted. Are you able to remove yourself so completely from what we face if we lose him?"

"Peter!" Simon said. "You misunderstand me. Yes, I was a Zealot, believing nothing was so important as our independence and seeing all methods of attaining it as expedient. But having met Jesus, I sensed that perhaps there were more important freedoms. Having been with him these three years, I now know that political freedom, which I still think is valid, is not nearly so important as our relationships with God and with one another. I am grateful I no longer have to sustain that angry, fighting spirit that was such a disturbing part of me but can live in peace. I have confidence that all that is important is in God's hands. Of course, I know what it will mean to us if we lose him. It's just that it seems inevitable, especially after these three days. It's really only a matter of time. And it does distress me to hear him predict that it is only two days away."

"I'm sorry, Simon," Peter apologized. "I always have been quicker with my tongue than with my head."

"Apology accepted," Simon responded. Then he continued, "It's not easy to accept the fact of Jesus leaving us. I can't imagine how we'll manage without him. But the signs of intrigue surround us. We cannot be blind to that; obviously Jesus isn't. And I have great concern about Judas. We used to talk a great deal about our hopes and dreams for our nation. Lately we have had little to say to each other. He seems to have withdrawn from us, to have turned inside himself. Something has happened to him. I hate to say such a thing about one of our circle, but I think we should watch him."

"You think he would turn on us?" questioned Peter.

"I don't know. But I noticed some bitterness in some of our last conversations, particularly after Jesus let us know he is our Messiah."

"But that is good news."

"Yes," agreed Simon, "to those of us who believe it. But there have been many false messiahs. Perhaps Judas' faith is weak."

Coming into sight of Lazarus' house and longing for the warmth of friendship they knew they would find there, they quickened their pace.

In the meantime the chief priests and elders of the people made their way to Caiaphas' palace. This man held all the power of the Jewish religious world. Both presiding officer of the Sanhedrin and high priest with Rome's approval, he commanded the highest position in Judaism and had direct access to Roman legal agencies. Not only did he have power and position, but it was his nature to be shrewd and calculating. If anyone could make things happen, Caiaphas could.

Though many expressed the need to stop Jesus' work, and some ideas as to how to accomplish this were debated, it all came to nothing. Not one of them was willing to take any risks with Passover upon them. It was much too dangerous. The people would riot, and then the situation would be worse because Rome would have to suppress the rebellion. It could only lead to a more unendurable political situation than now existed.

And so they agreed, "Not during the feast," but at some other time after the pilgrims had returned to their homes and the city had settled itself into its normal routine. The situation would be manageable then.

CHAPTER FIVE

Bethany

It was well past midday. Jesus and the twelve were guests in the home of Simon the jar merchant, who had once carried the stigma of leprosy. Jesus had healed him, and he was no longer condemned to wandering aimlessly away from towns and villages, a certain distance from other people, crying out the dreaded and embarrassing warning, "Unclean! Unclean!" Along with his health, his family and his business had long since been restored to him. He was happy again. Now he wanted to extend his hospitality to the man who had saved his life.

His successful jar business provided him with a magnificent house. Built of squared stone, which only the well-to-do could afford, it had the same type of sturdy construction as Lazarus' house. Today Simon entertained his guests in the summer room, which opened onto a courtyard. A date palm, two walnut trees, some sycamore, and several almond trees that were now white-shrouded in heavy blossom grew in that space. The flautist Simon had engaged to provide soft background music in honor of his beloved guest played softly so that the melancholy, haunting strains of mid-Eastern music floated through the rooms. The meal had been sumptuous, consisting of quail, fish, a lentil stew, cucumbers and tiny onions. They feasted on nuts, figs, apple slices, and fried honey cakes afterward to give a sweet contrast to the main course. Now, after eating such a hearty meal, the diners felt drowsy and conversation had lagged considerably. The music enticed them to sleepy reverie.

Maria entered the room almost soundlessly without disturbing the aura of peace. She moved so quietly that no one had even been aware of her leaving earlier, when she went to get her gift for Jesus. She returned carrying an alabaster jar of very expensive, pure nard. Before anyone realized what she was about to do, she broke the jar and poured the ointment over Jesus' head. Gently she massaged his head, not allowing any of the precious nard to be wasted. The disciples looked on in dismay. Judas found his tongue first, and his sharp words cut through the pleasant atmosphere.

"Why was this ointment wasted?" he harshly criticized Maria. "It could have been sold for three hundred denarii, and the money given to the poor."

But Jesus said, "Why do you trouble her? For she has done a beautiful thing to me. You always have the poor with you, but you will not always have me. Of a truth, I tell you that wherever this gospel is preached in the whole world, what she has done will be told in memory of her."

Judas turned away from his Master and stalked out of the room.

Unlike other times that he had absented himself from the group, Judas did not soon return. He had a mission. He had finally set his mind on the course he must take. There would be no second thoughts this time. He knew the chief priests were still trying to find a way to arrest Jesus, and he knew where he could find them.

Judas' disenchantment with Jesus had finally become complete. The wonderful new day he had envisioned for the future with Jesus as their glorious leader had wisped away. Satan had so twisted his thinking that Judas completely forgot how intrigued he had once been with the idea of a new age for Israel. He had always recognized the necessity for change. Now, however, when he thought of it in terms of Jesus' teachings about a new order, he could not tolerate the idea.

Judas was a great believer in the law and established religious traditions; he believed in the old order. In old order thinking one entered the kingdom of God through legalistic obedience to laws, while in the new order one gained entrance to the kingdom by obeying God's laws in the light of God's love. Judas had hoped the new age would come through the channels of law and sacred tradition and the restoration of Israel as it was in King David's time—old order thinking. He didn't see where love entered into it. Jesus taught that love tempers justice and transcends all else. Jesus believed they should live by something greater than law and tradition. He taught that a better kingdom than David's was available to all. This was all too much for Judas.

Now Judas was faced with a choice. He could either become part of the kingdom promised by Jesus and leave behind the old Judaism, or he could remain faithful to the established religious and social order he loved so much and abandon Jesus. Judas had become so entrenched in the old order of things that he could not see that sometimes reform is necessary in order that the best may emerge. He was an old wineskin unable to accommodate the energy of the new wine. He could see some good in Jesus' teaching; he could see the possibilities of a better way of life. But the old was still too much a part of him.

It frightened him to think that if the things Jesus taught really caught on and grew over the years, it could mean the end of Judaism as he knew it. Such drastic changes could not be tolerated. He could not see the more likely possibility that the old way would become more vital with the infusion of the love ethic that Jesus taught. He chose, therefore, that the new should die in order that the old might continue to live. He chose to aid Jesus' enemies to attain that end. Jesus must be silenced. Jesus wanted to change their way of life; he didn't want to be their king. In Judas' mind it was all wrong, but now he had the power to do something about it.

With dark purpose, yet justified by the expediency of his decision, Judas found the chief priests once again gathered in the house of Caiaphas. Of recent days such gatherings had been frequent. Judas had made it a point to know this against the possibility of his need to approach them.

The chief priests were not really surprised to see Judas when a servant ushered him into their presence. Their informants had indicated that Judas had apparently withdrawn from his circle of companions. He generally stayed behind the others and did not participate in their discussions. He appeared rather sullen most of the time. This had prompted them to believe that he might possibly be the first within the close circle to realize that Jesus was not all he claimed to be. If this should happen, he might somehow prove useful to them one day. So they waited in anticipation for him to speak, eager to hear how he might be of use to them.

Judas wasted no time. He didn't really like being here in spite of his negative feelings and purposeful resolve. He wanted to have the ugly business behind him.

"What will you give me if I deliver him to you?" There was no easing into the matter, no mincing of words.

"Not so fast," Asa said. "How do you propose to do this in the midst of Passover?"

"I will find a way, a time when he is alone. You will just have to trust me if you really want him because only I will know when and where that might be. There is no other way with so many people about these days."

Knowing that Judas spoke reality, and having already deliberated at length, the chief priests had no further need to discuss the matter. They agreed together to act at last, these powerful men who feared the power they sensed in this one peaceful man.

"We will give you thirty pieces of silver."

"Agreed."

Tucking the leather coin pouch into the girdle in his cloak, Judas turned quickly and walked out of the room.

The chief priests exchanged amazed glances. It had been easier than they possibly could have anticipated. Surely God himself had delivered Jesus into their hands. Of all the ideas they had discussed to take Jesus, betrayal by one of his own disciples had never been an option for them.

"He must have some deeper purpose in betraying his Master. It certainly wasn't for money," observed Asa. "I expected the price for Jesus to be much higher, especially from one of his own disciples."

"Obviously money was not an issue for him," Joram concurred. I had heard he was somewhat greedy. I never would have expected him to accept such a paltry sum."

As Judas left the house of conspiracy, he breathed a deep sigh, knowing that he had finally set the process in motion. Now he must return before his companions began to wonder about his whereabouts. He hurried back to Bethany, thinking as he went about what opportunities for betrayal might present themselves in the next few days. He wasn't sure, however, that what he felt was a sense of satisfaction.

By the time he returned, the others had already returned to Lazarus' house. Tomorrow they would celebrate the Feast of Unleavened Bread, so tonight marked the ceremony in which the head of the house would purify the dwelling of all leaven. As he came near he could see the movement of light through the windows. As unobtrusively as possible he slipped into the room where the others had gathered and dropped noiselessly to the floor.

Looking across the room he saw Mary, Jesus' mother, watching him. He dropped his eyes, accused by his own shame in her presence. He didn't know when she might have arrived, only that she was expected.

The flickering candle cast eerie shadows about the room as Lazarus poked into all the corners. He bent to look into the earthen jars and ran his hand along the shelves that lined one wall of the kitchen. Moving from one room to another, anywhere that food may have been carried, he searched carefully, solemnly intoning the ritualistic prayer, "Blessed art Thou, Jehovah, our God, King of the universe, who has sanctified us by Thy commandments and commanded us to remove the leaven."

In the kitchen he found some honey cakes and a jar almost empty of leaven because his sisters, knowing Passover was upon them, had not bothered to replenish their low supply. All of these things, plus all the crumbs from the floor, he then took to the stone oven in the kitchen and burned. As soon as he accomplished this, he ended this annual ceremony with the prescribed prayer, "All leaven which perchance remains in my domain and which has escaped my observation shall be destroyed and be like unto the dust of the earth."

Lazarus blew out the candle and rejoined Maria and Martha and their guests. The evening meal having been eaten, all were in a very relaxed, though subdued, mood. Seventeen dined in Lazarus' house this night. Jesus and the twelve had been most welcome guests when they came to his house each night to escape Jerusalem. He understood that they should want to do so.

The confusion in the city that always accompanied the beginning of Passover made Jerusalem a very disquieting place to be. All the usual noise and congestion in the city increased many-fold by the gathering pilgrims and last-minute shoppers. The bartering and arguing, the shouting, the hustle and bustle of the bazaar—all this made that city impossible to endure for more than a few hours at a time. Jesus' week had been a very trying one even without all of that, and he needed the quiet to restore his mind and spirit.

The newcomer in the household that night was Mary from Nazareth. Her reunion with Jesus had been quietly touching. Though they exchanged few words, their embrace was warm and tender, expressing the love that existed between mother and son. Mary was content just to have her eldest son close at hand. However, something had dampened her joy. There were troubling undertones in the conversation that flowed around her during the mealtime.

Jesus broke the silence following the cleansing ceremony.

"The quiet here is refreshing, Lazarus. You have been most kind to welcome us into your home yet again. You are a good friend."

Lazarus was pleased that Jesus had felt free enough to come to his home at will, glad that his home was large enough to accommodate so many. He loved Jesus, would do anything for him, and wished he could do more for him.

"I am happy to be of service. The time you spent in Jerusalem this week has been difficult with so many contriving arguments with you. You needed a reprieve in a quiet place. I hope our home in Bethany can continue to be your haven from the storms of the city."

"I thank you too, Lazarus," Mary said. "And I'm most grateful to you because what you said is true, that a quiet place is what Jesus and the others need right now."

She looked at Jesus, loving care soft in her eyes. "Son, you look tired. I wish that you wouldn't have to go into Jerusalem again. It upsets me to see you so worn out."

She patted his hand and sighed, knowing that her words fell on deaf ears. Jesus could never do the easy thing. She felt a sadness she could not explain; moreover she knew she was not alone in this feeling.

Jesus did not respond, only looked at her, compassion plainly written in his face.

"All Jerusalem is full tonight, it seems." Matthew broke the uncomfortable silence that had settled in following Mary's gentle chiding. "Any additional pilgrims coming into the city will find it impossible to secure lodging."

"Yes," agreed Lazarus. "When I was there again today, I talked to a man who had come from Egypt. He had his wife with him and his twelve-year-old son. Like so many of these pilgrims he had been saving for years so he could come here for Passover. He wanted his son to celebrate the first Passover of his manhood in Jerusalem. But he had difficulty finding a place to stay. He had been looking for hours by the time I met him and was extremely discouraged. I would have gladly brought them here if that would have helped."

"It's too bad that the city's boundaries are extended only as far as Bethphage. Many people even here in Bethany would gladly offer lodging," Martha said.

"Well, fortunately, I happened to know of a place where they could go. Joseph, the potter who lives near the Ephraim Gate, had just told me he could take two or even three people. I sent them there, and that poor man couldn't thank me enough."

Judas then observed, "The Tower of Antonia is bulging with Rome's soldiers. They seem to be everywhere. Besides causing additional overcrowding in our city, the very sight of them is repulsive. They are a curse on us!"

"Love your enemies, my son," Jesus chided gently.

"How can I love my enemies?" Judas was angry, red-faced. "Love the Romans? They've never done anything to merit my love. They rule over us brutally, totally without mercy. Who are they to think they can control our lives? They take our money; their soldiers watch over our shoulders and molest our women;

they defile our country with their pagan ways. How can you tolerate this abomination? Forget all the teaching and healing and rule us. You could call down the angels, and Rome wouldn't stand a chance. Then we could have our nation back and worship in peace and without fear!"

If any taut nerves had relaxed, Judas' outburst undid it all. His anger overruled any sensitivity he might have had for the mood of the somber group. Nor did he consider that his actions would soon transform the unease of those around him to bitter anguish.

Peter turned to Nathanael in disgust, murmuring, "He's at it again. Do you suppose he will ever grow weary of his anger?"

Once again Jesus' eyes registered deepened sadness, and disappointment was there too. He had tried so hard to make his disciples understand God's love, that it was different from the way humans understood love. Judas was apparently blind to the truth. What more could he have said or done that would have brought peace and understanding to this troubled man?

Wearily he responded, "Judas, I have already told you, my kingdom is not of this world. It would solve nothing for me to become your king. How can I make you understand that God loves all people? The only way to have real peace is for his love to be in the hearts of all people so that they will love one another. When that happens, there will be no need for kings and kingdoms."

Judas became sullen. He could not understand why Jesus didn't seem to be aware of his predicament, and he blamed him for his own predicament. It was a hateful situation. He could not agree with anyone less; they were in diametric opposition. He had no further argument.

Everyone else felt uncomfortable. Silence once again permeated the room. The somber mood that had been only a vague feeling now pervaded the group.

Lazarus looked at Jesus, whose tiredness was etched deeply in his face, and at the disciples who seemed restless. Judas still bristled with unspent anger and frustration, his upper lip twitching. James and John stood off by themselves in low conversation. Peter had begun pacing the floor. Lazarus knew only too well what had been happening all week, and so he understood everyone's confusion. Life had changed for them rapidly and drastically. Mary had been on the road for these past four days. Travel weary, she needed a good night's rest. It was obvious that Judas' outburst had wounded her deeply. Tears ran down her cheeks, unchecked.

Lazarus rose and suggested it was time to retire for the night.

"The sun set long ago, my friends. Tomorrow begins Passover. I hope that you will all find rest in my house tonight."

Gratefully his guests went off to their beds, bidding Lazarus a good night. When he was alone, he stood thinking that never had there been a more disconsolate gathering in this room. It was such a radical contrast to all those joyous times when they had shared meals with Jesus and listened in rapt attention to his teaching and his stories. Shaking himself physically, as though trying to rid himself of an uncomfortable burden, he attempted to throw off the heavy melancholy. After extinguishing the candle, he wearily sought his own bed.

Chapter Six

Premonitions

Mary was vaguely aware of a cool breeze whispering across her face. Something, she wasn't sure what, had wakened her, although it wasn't quite light yet. She had no desire to get up. A certain uneasiness filled her, making her hesitant to face the day. Besides, it felt so good to lie still, cuddled cozily in the soft blanket, and just allow herself to drift back to sleep. The thought alone that she would not be traveling today made her feel lazy. She felt relief at sleeping in the quietness of a house, lying on a bed instead of in the midst of the noise of a busy inn. She had rested on a pallet on the floor for the previous three nights. She sighed deeply and closed her eyes.

Just as she dozed off again, she heard the crowing of the cock. Now she knew that he had awakened her earlier. He must have been intoxicated with the feeling of spring in the air for he kept crowing, again and again. Everyone within hearing distance would have to greet the new dawn and be glad for it besides, if that rooster would have his way. But regardless of his insistence

Mary's unquenched weariness won out, and she soon dropped off to sleep.

She dozed a long while. When she woke again, the sun streamed in through the window, and she could smell unleavened bread baking. It was unmistakable—definitely bread, but without that yeasty aroma. It was the fourteenth day of the month of Nisan, and Passover would begin at sundown. She knew Maria and Martha must be preparing for the big event. Feeling guilty about oversleeping, she rose, quickly splashed her face with cold water from the basin beside her bed, and put on fresh clothes. She appreciated not having to wear dusty travel garments yet another day.

In spite of her inner uneasiness she felt cheerful in her apricot-colored robe and pale blue girdle. She slipped on a pair of black leather slippers, ran a comb through her hair, and arranged her head covering. Feeling even a bit perky, she went to greet her hostesses.

Martha was just removing the unleavened bread from the oven as Mary entered the room. She smiled warmly as she greeted her.

"Good morning."

"Good morning, Martha."

"Did you sleep well?" Martha inquired. "You do look refreshed."

"Yes, but I am ashamed at having slept so late."

"No matter. You needed the rest after that long journey down from Nazareth. How would you like something to eat? It is many hours yet until the feasting time this evening."

Mary accepted the offer, and as she sat eating her corn porridge and honey, she watched Martha at work preparing the food for the big meal that evening. Martha was a lovely woman with her thick, dark hair escaping her head covering and falling in waves around her face, and her brown eyes so dark as to appear black. She had the beginnings of worry lines between her eyebrows, and her hands were obviously those of a woman who spent much time in the kitchen.

"Martha, you do love to make a feast. Here you've been working since dawn, no doubt, and you still work energetically and cheerfully." Mary's thoughts turned to spoken words.

"Oh, yes. I find it very satisfying to delight my guests, even more so since Jesus had that little talk with me."

"Little talk?"

"Yes, didn't he tell you?"

"No," Mary said sadly. "We've had no time to ourselves since I arrived. In any case, he probably wouldn't have told me of this 'little talk.'"

"Well, not too long ago he was here with the twelve, and I tried to serve a large meal to them. I got more agitated with every minute that passed because Maria wasn't helping me. I became so upset I finally went and asked Jesus to tell her to help me. I didn't think it was right for her to leave me to work alone while she sat at Jesus' feet listening to him as though she were a man. He just looked at me, not in a condemning way, but there was no doubt in my mind that he thought me a bit foolish. He simply said that I was anxious and troubled about many things. 'Maria has chosen the good part, and that will not be taken away from her.'

"At first I resented it, but then I realized that he was right. I wasn't upset with Maria just because she wasn't helping me, but also because I wanted to be there listening to Jesus too. But someone had to do the work. I felt the responsibility of being a proper hostess. So after that I changed my priorities and gave more time to the really important things in life."

"But you still entertain with enthusiasm," noted Mary.

"Yes, I haven't given up that pleasure. The change was in my attitude. First, I realized that I can't make Maria, or anyone else, attach the same importance to things as I do. She is entitled to her own choices, and just because they aren't the same as mine doesn't make them wrong. Second, I found that if I relaxed the pressure on myself and made things simpler, I had more time and energy for my guests. I actually enjoy entertaining more than I did before. Just realizing those two things has made it possible for me to live without the anxiety Jesus said I had."

"It is good that you could listen to him, Martha, and learn. You seem well contented with your life."

Conversation lulled and the quietness grew. It dawned on Mary that she sensed the quietness of an empty house, and she commented, "No one seems to be around this morning. Did Lazarus go to Jerusalem with Jesus?"

"No, and Jesus left only about an hour before you got up. Peter and John left much earlier. I heard them asking Jesus where he wanted them to prepare for the eating of the Passover meal. I thought it rather strange when he told them they should look for a man carrying a jar of water—can you imagine that?—and follow him to a certain house. They were to speak to the man of the house, telling him that the Teacher said his time was at hand and he wanted to keep the Passover at his house with his disciples. He said the man would give them his upper room. What do you suppose he meant, 'my time is at hand?'"

"It's hard to know. He seemed so withdrawn last evening and downcast."

Mary wondered at the somber mood of her son, his quietness, and his restlessness. Concern about his depression of spirit shadowed her whole being. She felt oppressed by gloom, and she didn't want to feel this way. One person brooding over her anxieties could easily dampen the enjoyment of those around her no matter how festive the occasion. She determined to throw off these black shadows and asked Martha again, "Has Lazarus gone with them? Oh, I forgot. You already answered that. I'm not thinking too well this morning."

"That's all right. It's quite understandable. Lazarus is just outside inspecting our little lamb again, making sure there aren't some blemishes he missed. He chose a beautiful yearling for the feast. It's a fat one, and I don't think there will be any problem in having it certified. All of us will enjoy plenty of good eating this evening." Martha spoke as she busied herself with preparing the wine for that evening, carefully measuring out two parts of water to three parts of wine.

After a moment she continued speaking of Lazarus. "He is anxious to get going. He loves to be in the city when the crowds are so large and cosmopolitan; the excitement enlivens him. He has a great interest in what is happening in other parts of the world and learns much from the pilgrims. Remember what he told us last night about his experience yesterday? Such contacts make him feel that he is really a part of the whole world. The time passes quickly for him."

"This is unusual, isn't it?" Framed as a question, it was really an observation. "I can't say that I know of many who think beyond their own home village."

Maria's appearance interrupted them. She came in from the courtyard, her arms full of almond blossom branches, which she arranged in large urns to bring some springtime fragrance and freshness into the house. Maria was much younger than Martha, with the same dark hair and eyes, but something about her eyes drew one's attention immediately. Like deep crystalline pools, they suggested an inner depth of thought that her lively manner almost belied, and her mouth seemed to be perpetually smiling. She had a bounce in her walk that revealed her zest for life.

"Good morning, Mary," she lilted. "I'm so glad you're up and we can talk. Did you sleep well?"

"Yes, I slept very well indeed, thank you."

When Maria had arranged the flowers to her satisfaction, she came over to sit by Mary, picking up a bowl of water and a large handful of dandelion greens on the way.

"Has Martha told you what happened on the first day of the week?"

"No, we haven't gotten to that yet," Martha said.

"Oh, but how could you not think of it right away?" Maria questioned. "I think it's so exciting," she continued, without waiting for any response. "We were in Jerusalem making final arrangements with Elian for our Passover in Jerusalem. You should have been here then, Mary. You would have seen how popular Jesus is in Jerusalem. Everyone treated him like a king. Well, almost everyone. And he looked like one, sitting on that donkey so straight and majestic. They must have waved hundreds of palm branches, to say nothing of all the palm fronds that were laid on the ground for him to ride over. Some people even laid their own cloaks on the ground in front of him. Can there be any doubt now that people want Jesus for our king?"

Maria was so enthusiastic that Mary could easily visualize the events of that day. The palm branches said so much to her. After all, they symbolized victory. The people acknowledged Jesus as their victorious king. Could it be that now the Jewish people would know victory over Rome and be free once and for all of outside rule? The palm branches were Jesus' royal banners, carried before him by loyal subjects, heralding his entry into the city he had conquered in peace, the beautiful city of Jerusalem.

Maria's voice brought her back to the present. This woman, usually so serious-minded, was starry eyed and bubbling with excitement. "And the way everyone was shouting, 'Hosanna!' My heart pounded and tears came to my eyes. 'Hosanna! Hosanna! Hail to the King!' everyone was shouting." Maria was caught up in her own enthusiasm. "The festal exhilaration was contagious. I could not help but join in, even more so when someone handed palm branches to us. It was such a celebration. After all, Jesus is our king, whether or not he wears the purple and sits on a throne of gold in a royal palace. The people love him and will do anything for him. I know this is true."

"It was exciting to be in the midst of all that jubilation. And it does sound wonderful, doesn't it?" Martha agreed with a faraway look in her eyes. "To be independent again—not to have to pay taxes to Caesar; not to have Roman soldiers roaming our streets all the time. It's a most satisfying thought indeed."

She paused, thinking how different life would be, then forcefully brought herself back to reality. Turning to Maria, she gently chided, "I can't believe you are saying these things, Maria. This is so unlike you, to be caught up in popular sentiment even when it goes against Jesus' teaching. It sounds as though you really believe that Jesus means to overthrow Roman rule, to become the king of a new nation of Israel. But that is not to be. You heard what he said last night, and what he's said before about his true kingdom."

Maria nodded in agreement, her jubilant mood noticeably wilted. "Yes, of course you are right. I do know better than that, but the growing fervor of the crowd was just too difficult to resist. And you just said yourself how wonderful it would be if it were to happen."

"Yes, I admit that I too have thoughts of how wonderful that would be," Martha conceded. "But we know that none of the many stories Jesus told about the kingdom of God had anything to do with overthrowing Rome and reestablishing Israel. The stories Jesus told were about a different kind of kingdom, more permanent, more beautiful, not of this earth at all."

"But I think it is of this earth, Martha," argued Maria. "Or at least it begins on this earth, within us. Remember the story Jesus told about the soil?" She turned to Mary, thinking that perhaps she wouldn't have heard it. "He told how a farmer went out to plant seed, and as he did some of the seed fell along the path where the birds came and ate it up; some fell on rocky ground where it couldn't grow properly because there was not enough soil; some fell among thorny bushes and was choked out as soon as it came up; but some fell on good soil and grew up to be healthy and plentiful. He explained how this was like God's kingdom.

"The word of God is the seed. Whenever anyone hears it but does not understand it, Satan comes and takes it away, just as the birds ate the seed along the path in the story. When someone hears the word and accepts it but does not allow it to take root in his heart, he falls away easily when trials or persecution come along. This is the rocky ground he talked about. When someone hears the word but cares more about other things, those other things choke out God's word just as the thorns choked out the seed in the story. Those who hear God's word and understand it are like the good soil, and they produce much good fruit, and it begins right here on earth."

"I was in Capernaum at that time and heard Jesus tell this story," Mary stated. "It seemed to me he was saying the kingdom of God is something that can be within each of us even now."

Maria nodded. "I think so too. I believe God wants to set up his kingdom in the heart of each person, which is really better than having a new and free kingdom of Israel. If we all would let God rule in our hearts, then the whole earth would be a peaceful kingdom. And Martha is right; this has nothing to do with what the world thinks a kingdom is."

Maria finished washing the dandelion greens and looked around for something else to do. She picked up a large basket of apples and began paring them, working slowly and pensively. Mary took a knife to help her. As they continued talking, they pared and chopped the apples, to which Martha would add chopped dates, pomegranate, nuts, cinnamon sticks, and wine to make the charosheth that would be an important part of the meal that evening.

Mary thought as she chopped apples. These two women had been exposed to Jesus' teachings quite a bit, not only because of what they heard whenever he taught in Jerusalem, but even more because they had the benefit of private conversations with him. He loved this family so he came to visit them as often as he could. Evidently his words had had a great effect on them; they had fallen on "good soil." They knew that the kingdom Jesus talked about was not an earthly one. She wondered how many of Jesus' followers thought so deeply about what he said or understood even half so well as Maria and Martha obviously did.

Lazarus came in, ending Mary's thoughts.

"Good morning, Mary," he said. He too asked about her night. Satisfied that she had slept comfortably, he announced, "We must leave for Jerusalem by noon. Simon and his family will be here by then to go with us. Many will travel the road today, and I would like us to be in the first group to come to the altar." With those words he went back outside.

Mary could hear the lamb bleating in the courtyard. *Poor little thing*, she thought, *so soon to die and so young.*

When Lazarus had left, Martha picked up the conversation again. "As you know Jesus has come here with his disciples each night, and they have told us about some of the things that have happened. Lazarus has been in Jerusalem each day, and he always tells us what he hears too. We were there ourselves one day. Jesus never discusses these things. He keeps his thoughts to himself."

"Yes," agreed Maria. "He is always so tired when he comes. You saw how he was last night, Mary. I have never seen such sadness in a man's eyes. He comes, eats a little supper, and after inquiring about our day, retires for the night. He and the others are always gone in the morning before first light."

"It isn't hard to understand his discouragement and fatigue," Martha added. "The day of his coming so triumphantly into Jerusalem, he and the disciples went to the temple to pray. Jesus became so angry with the moneychangers there that he upset all their tables and released the lambs and doves they were selling. What a sight to behold—doves all aflutter overhead; the lambs running about in utter confusion, bleating petulantly; coins rolling all over the ground with those greedy little men scrambling around on their knees, trying to recover as much as possible; and the disciples watching in amazement as Jesus yelled at those merchants!"

Maria laughed, a soft little trill of musical laughter, and exclaimed, "How funny to see grown men crawling in the dust like little boys playing marbles in the sand!"

Martha agreed with her sister, but she wasn't smiling. "It wasn't very funny to those men, though. They were humiliated and very angry. Jesus was angry too. He was disgusted with their unfair business practices that we all know so well. They station themselves in the temple where we go to pray, and where they teach us to be honest and treat one another fairly, doing just the opposite themselves."

Mary knew what they meant by unfair business practices. The temple tax, half a shekel a year, had to be paid in temple shekels. This meant that people coming to Jerusalem from all over the world for Passover needed to change their own money to these special shekels, and the moneychangers took unfair advantage by charging exorbitant exchange rates. They were rich men because of this and other irregularities. Mary also knew that they greatly overcharged their customers for the sacrificial animals they sold. A dove that cost one drachma anywhere else, cost five shekels in the temple—about twenty times as much. Those who lived around Jerusalem knew this and could bring their own animals, but even then the greedy temple officials often refused to pass them for inspection. Those who came from far-off places were caught unawares when they went to buy their sacrificial lambs. No one could really do anything about this situation, because it occurred under the control and with the blessing of Annas, the former high priest and father-in-law of Caiaphas, the present high priest.

Martha continued, "The thing I fear most is the anger of Annas. He will not forget this act of Jesus. He lost money and he lost face. He was personally hurt and he won't forget that. He will just add it to his list of grievances against Jesus. Did you know while the people were proclaiming Jesus king, the chief priests asked Jesus to put a stop to it? He wouldn't, and I know that this will be yet another weapon for Annas to use against Jesus. Annas and Caiaphas are afraid to do anything right now because the people so obviously love Jesus that they would never allow any harm to come to him, but they will not forget these things. They are just biding their time. I know it."

"What else do you know about these days?" Mary hoped for news of a different kind—news that wouldn't make her feel so uneasy and frightened but would perhaps even reassure her.

"Well, the other day he made the Pharisees very angry." Maria answered Mary's question, though certainly not in the way she had hoped. "That was the day Martha and I happened to be at the temple for our Passover devotions. While we were there a great crowd gathered in the Court of the Gentiles, so we stayed to see what it was all about. Some Pharisees, Sadducees, and chief priests clustered around Jesus. They waved their arms about, obviously excited and upset. Nicodemus was there, and Simon, our neighbor here in Bethany, and also Joseph—I believe he is from Arimathea. They and some others stood aside, not entering into the argument, yet they appeared to be very interested in the conversation."

"But how did Jesus make them all so angry?" Mary asked in some desperation.

Maria continued, apparently not having heard Mary's tone in her question. "They asked him where he got all his authority to do the things he has been doing. You know, his teaching about the kingdom, the healings, even the forgiveness of sins. But instead of answering their questions, he asked them whether the baptism of John was from heaven or from men. When they couldn't answer him, he did not answer them either. Instead he told them a story about a man planting a vineyard, then leaving the country, and the servants stealing the vineyard and murdering the man's son. You know, I think those Pharisees knew he was alluding to them somehow. They were extremely angry but without argument."

Martha picked up the story. "Then they tried to badger him into committing treason against Rome. They asked him if it was lawful under God to pay taxes to Caesar. Even I knew that if he said no, the Romans would arrest him. If he said yes, he would have been in trouble with the Sadducees. He was trapped, or so we thought. But he merely asked them to show him a coin and tell him whose likeness was on it. Of course, since it was Caesar's, that meant it belonged to him. Jesus responded that they should pay to Caesar whatever rightfully belonged to him, and give to God the things that are God's. They were smoldering from that response and totally frustrated that their attempt to trap him failed so miserably."

Maria nodded. "The questions they asked were very difficult. It seemed to us that no matter how he answered them, they would have destroyed him. Yet he always had the final word, and they just looked like a bunch of jackals. They asked him so many unanswerable questions, but he gave brilliant responses. Finally, I guess they decided not to pursue such an unproductive course any longer and gave it up. But you can be sure that this temporary setback will not deter them. They will eventually find a way to use all of these things as evidence against him. It frightens me. They won't give up until they have taken him away from us."

"It frightens me too," Martha said, "and his accusations against the Pharisees make it even more frightening. I think I'll never forget that as long as I live. Just hearing those scathing words coming from Jesus knotted my heart with a fear I've never felt before. I don't think it will ever loosen its grip on me."

"What in the world did he say that would be so frightening?" The situation deteriorated from bad to worse, and Mary's uneasiness rapidly increased to a fear that matched Martha's. What he said she just couldn't imagine.

Maria spoke for her sister because the memory of that strong fear made it difficult for her to speak rationally. She repeated as best she could what their startled ears had heard that day at the temple. "'The scribes and Pharisees are in authority over you concerning the law, so practice and observe whatever they tell you. But do not do what they do. They do not practice what they teach. They force others to carry heavy burdens that they themselves refuse to carry. Everything they do is for show so others will think them great. They love to sit in the place of honor at feasts and in the best seats in the synagogues. They take pride in being recognized in the marketplace and being called rabbi by men.' Then he said to them, 'Woe to you, scribes and Pharisees, you are hypocrites!' Imagine that—hypocrites!—our great teachers, the elite of our people, keepers of our souls. 'You refuse to enter into the kingdom of heaven yourselves, nor will you allow those who would enter to go in.' He told them they concentrated on the little unimportant things of life and neglected the important." Maria's voice dropped almost to a whisper. "He called them 'whited sepulchres,' clean on the outside but filthy within."

Mary sat there, feeling the cold chill of fear growing in her until it nearly overwhelmed her. The uneasiness she had felt, and that she had sensed in the others, settled in a nauseous lump in the pit of her stomach. The feeling rose into her throat so that she thought she was going to be sick. Intense fatigue overtook her. She ached, body and soul. As all this overtook her, she thought, *I wonder why they have told me all these terrible things. Surely they must know how frightened it would make me to hear that my son is in mortal danger. They are usually loving and thoughtful, yet this morning they have spared me nothing. I think I must get out of this room.*

"I feel the need of rest," Mary told them, "and would like to lie down awhile."

The two sisters looked at Mary, now pale and obviously shaken. They immediately realized what they had done to her. They had been so caught up in apprising her of recent events that they had not considered Mary's feelings. Neither of them could believe they had been so thoughtless and could think of nothing to say beyond a weak but genuine "I'm sorry." In chagrined silence they watched her walk slowly from the room.

Mary lay down on her bed, hoping to fall asleep, but after a short time decided it was useless. She could not keep her thoughts from racing. Pictures and words crowded together in her mind, each one relentlessly capturing her attention—Jesus riding a donkey—Jesus angry—palm branches—birds beating their wings in frantic flight—money jangling on a stone floor—red-faced Pharisees—taxes to Caesar. And through it all were interwoven the words Messiah—Messiah—Messiah, the warp of the whole tapestry of Jesus' life. Though no one had mentioned that word, she knew that this was an important consideration in all that had been happening. Her concern for Jesus' safety rapidly increased.

She got up from her bed and began removing the few things she had in her travel bundle to the small chest in her room, making small work for herself. She needed activity more than rest, but her unpacking took so little time, and no thought, that it didn't help. She had only one other robe, two tunics, and some undergarments to put away. She went to see if she could do anything more to help in the kitchen, but Maria and Martha weren't anywhere to be found.

She decided to go for a walk. After changing from her house slippers to sandals, she stepped into the bright sunshine. All the beautiful sights, sounds, and smells of a refreshing spring day surrounded the large stone house. The singing of the birds lifted her spirits somewhat. The clean, fresh color of the shrubs and trees, wearing a lovely pale green that was seen only in spring, delighted her eyes. She slowly walked through the garden, admiring the delicate beauty of the white calla lilies that contrasted sharply with the deep purple of the irises nearby. She soon found herself wishing that Jesus were here to walk with her and reassure her.

They had had such a short time together last evening, and the joy of reunion had been dulled by deep disappointment. He had told her that he would be with his disciples for this Passover. He told her it was necessary. The news hit her like a sharp blow, but she knew she would have to accept it. She tried not to show her disappointment, but it was there nevertheless. She made a great effort to console herself with the thought that there would be plenty of time later to visit with him. She could always celebrate the Passover with him another year. In this manner she had tried to talk herself out of her disappointment.

Mary looked up, surprised where her walk had taken her. The sepulcher where Lazarus had lain for four days had come into view. Jesus had restored life to him, and it disturbed the chief priests more than anything else he had done up to that point. She knew this because Lazarus himself had told her about the miracle. Understandably he wanted to share his story with anyone who cared to listen, but especially with Jesus' mother. And so she heard of this marvelous event almost as soon as she had arrived in his home.

Lazarus also said that after this unheard-of event, the priests really began to worry about the influence Jesus had on the people. After all, what person having the power to make dead people live couldn't be a powerful leader? The priests feared that this upstart from Nazareth would destroy the delicate balance that existed between the Romans and the Jews. As long as the Jews remained docile, at least outwardly, everything would continue to be all right. Jesus threatened this harmonious (though deceptively so) arrangement. The raising of Lazarus was one more thing that made Jesus a marked man. Mary knew their list had become rather lengthy.

Chapter Seven

Sacrifice

By the time Mary returned to the house, it was time to leave for Jerusalem. Someone had tied the little donkey by the outer door, his back already laden with the large baskets full of the food they had spent the morning preparing.

Mary entered the house in the midst of much activity and noise. She removed her dusty sandals and bathed her feet in the small tub kept near the door for that purpose. She found Martha packing still another basket with the silver wine cups they would need for the feast, carefully wrapping them in white linen napkins.

"Mary, where have you been?" Martha asked, surprised to see her come in from the outside instead of across the courtyard from her room. "We thought you were resting, though I'm not at all sure how you could have with all the noise we've been making."

"I went for a walk," Mary explained. "My mind was too wrought up after such disturbing talk. I need to keep myself busy with other things. What must be done yet before we are ready to leave?"

"Nothing. This is the last of it," Martha responded. "I hope our poor little donkey doesn't complain too much when we add this to what he's already carrying." She paused a moment, then looking carefully at Mary, she apologized once again. "I'm sorry that we upset you. We should have known all of this would be immensely disturbing to you; it was hard even for us as we realized what was happening. We should never have burdened you, at least not with everything at once, and certainly not on this day of festivity. Please forgive us."

"Don't be too concerned, Martha. I'll be all right. Besides, I would have learned it all sooner or later, and perhaps it was better to hear it from you, who love him so much." Mary's words of assurance sounded braver in her ears than she really felt, but she held no grudge against her friends for speaking the truth to her, as difficult as it was to hear.

"Well, I do hope it doesn't spoil the rest of the day for you. As soon as Simon gets here, we can go."

Just at that moment the two women heard Lazarus greeting someone in the street. Knowing it must be Simon, they hurriedly gathered the last of their bundles and joined the others. Simon had brought two donkeys. He had packed one with baskets of food for the feast, as well as the things that would be needed for the night since they would not return to Bethany until the next day. The feasting usually lasted well into the dark hours of night.

On the other donkey sat Sara, Simon's wife, a frail woman who could not walk even the short distance of five miles to Jerusalem. Along with them were Matthias and Rebekah, Simon's son and daughter-in-law, and their children, young Simon, Leah, and James. The children twirled about excitedly, impatient to be getting on with the adventure. Glad to have them along, Mary knew that children brought special joy to festival times. They loved holidays and celebrations, and participated with all their energy, spreading their enthusiasm to everyone within reach. She missed her own grandchildren, and these children would help fill the void.

They started walking down the rocky street toward the main road that led to Jerusalem, joining the many pilgrims who were already headed in that direction. This was an important occasion, often a once-in-a-lifetime event, to be in Jerusalem to celebrate the most important of all festivals. The mood of the other pilgrims only intensified the mood of the two families. At times they burst into songs of praise, singing exuberantly, joyously.

The children found it difficult to maintain the slower, steady pace of their elders and often ran ahead, then back again to their parents. After they had been out of sight for longer than usual, Rebekah needed to admonish them when they returned not to stray too far away. "There are so many people, children, it would be easy to get lost in this crowd. Try to keep us in your sight all the time."

"Yes, Mama," they breathlessly responded. They were off again but not before Rebekah cautioned, "Be mindful of the tombstones. Remember how important it is that you must not touch them."

"Yes, Mama," came from far down the road.

The travelers would easily notice any tombstones that might be standing near the roadway. Long before this day, several weeks in fact, they had all been whitewashed to warn unwary strangers of their location. It would be most unfortunate for a pilgrim, filled with the anticipation of the Passover, to touch one of these tombstones even accidentally. That person, thus rendered unclean, would be unable to partake of the Passover feast.

Maria, who had been chatting with Sara, dropped back and waited for Martha and Mary to catch up.

"I've been thinking a lot about what we discussed this morning. You know, the kingdom Jesus talks about. Why isn't it possible for the Messiah to be both a spiritual and an earthly ruler?"

Mary gasped, startled at hearing her use the word *messiah.* She had lived with the idea that Jesus was the Messiah for all these years, but she had never breathed a word to anyone. She and Joseph used to speak of it together in awed, hushed tones, as one does when sharing a closely guarded secret shrouded in mystery. But this was no ordinary secret; it was supernatural, beyond human understanding. This knowledge that they had must remain with them until God himself chose to reveal it. After all, the Jews looked for a king, not a carpenter's son, to be their leader, so who would have believed them anyway?

Maria and Martha both noticed her reaction. Carefully Maria began to speak once more. "Is it possible for any to know him, and the Scriptures, and not understand that he is the Messiah? I know that for such a long time now we have been looking for another king as great as David who will rule us with righteousness and justice. If that were to happen, we would be supreme among the nations again instead of under the foot of another nation. But it has occurred to me that we are looking for the wrong kind of messiah. I began to think about this after Peter told me how he met Jesus.

"Remember, Martha, what he said? Andrew heard John the Baptist call Jesus the Lamb of God. Right after that Jesus invited him, and Philip who was with him, to visit him where he was staying. He talked to them for some hours. When they left him, they were convinced that Jesus was the Messiah. That's when Andrew brought his brother, Peter, to meet Jesus, telling him he had found the Messiah."

Maria paused for some moments, then continued reflectively, "And I keep thinking about that passage in Isaiah where it says the Spirit of God is upon him, and he is to bring good tidings to the afflicted and comfort to the brokenhearted. Jesus has been doing that all this time."

"Yes," Martha agreed quietly, "he has been doing that. He comforted my broken heart when Lazarus died."

"Tell me, Martha," Mary pleaded. "Tell me what he said, please."

Martha took a deep breath, then told her story, beginning with her hurt that Jesus had not come to them soon enough to prevent Lazarus' death.

"That day, when he finally came to us, I reproached him. We were so disappointed he hadn't come in time to heal Lazarus. But somehow I felt it still wasn't too late. I remember saying to him that even then God would grant whatever he would ask of him. When he said that Lazarus would rise again, I assumed he meant in the last resurrection. But he said a curious thing then—'I am the resurrection and the life; he who believes in me, though he die, yet shall he live, and whoever lives and believes in me shall never die.' He asked me if I believed this.

"As I thought about it, I began to understand something of what he was saying, that if he is the resurrection and the life, then he has the power to overcome death. Whatever that might mean for Lazarus and for us, I immediately knew in my heart that one with such power had to be of God. I told him that I believe he is the Christ, the Messiah, the Son of God, the one who came into the world as promised."

The women lapsed into pensive silence, each in her own way trying to comprehend the bold thoughts that had just been stated aloud.

Mary's own thoughts tumbled over themselves. *The Messiah—yes, Jesus was indeed the Messiah, the Promised One, the one sent to redeem Israel.* She knew that, and now some of Jesus' most faithful followers knew it too, had known it for some time, it seemed. But wouldn't Annas be happy to hear such an admission! It would be the one thing, above all the other complaints of the religious leaders of Jerusalem, that would ensure the demise of her son. The claim to messiahship would be construed as blasphemy, punishable by death. Not only that, but Israel's religious leaders did not want anything to bring political disaster on their nation. They knew that anyone claiming to be a king would be a threat to Caesar.

Already the Sanhedrin had begun its work of seeking Jesus to bring him to trial. She had heard of the WANTED notices the Sanhedrin had posted in an effort to bring Jesus to them. She occasionally heard tales of mockery. Even in his own home town of Nazareth they had once tried to kill him. How interesting that Maria should have mentioned the very passage Jesus had read in their synagogue on that awful day. She still didn't know how Jesus had escaped the angry crowd.

Mary remembered how, not so very long ago, she had tried to persuade Jesus not to go down into the city at this particular time. She knew the crowds would be large and that it would be much easier for harm to come to him. But he had closed his ears to her. One look into his sad eyes made her resolve not to add to his burdens by her own worried nagging, so she had let the matter drop. He had told her that this was something he had to do, and the set of his face, which she had seen before, told her it was no use to argue anyway.

That resolute look reminded her of the day he had first left Nazareth—*was it really only three years ago?* Just the day before that he had finished making a table for Jared, the potter, one of their neighbors. He was in great demand as a carpenter because he did such beautiful work. *He didn't charge enough though*, she thought. *He could have made an excellent living as a carpenter.* The wealthy were willing to pay handsomely for his beautifully crafted creations. Instead he chose to be of service to his friends in Nazareth, building what they needed, charging little because that was all they could afford.

She really couldn't complain though. After all, her family had wanted for nothing they really needed because Jesus worked so hard on their behalf. *And besides*, she reminded herself, *you know very well he wasn't here to be a carpenter or to get rich; God had a plan for him, still has, and all things will work out according to that plan.*

It was hard giving him up, though she knew he wasn't hers to give. That day that he left home to begin his work was difficult beyond her imagining. Early that morning he had delivered the table to Jared. Upon returning home, he had placed the coins in her hand and folded her fingers around them. Then, clasping her fist in both of his work-calloused hands, he made his earth-shattering announcement.

"It is time for me to leave Nazareth, Mother. I must now be doing the things my Father sent me here to do. There is some money in the old cracked water jar in the far corner of the wood shop. Every time I was paid for a job, I put a coin in there against this day. James and the other boys are good workmen. You will be well cared for."

"Oh, Jesus, must you go away? Can't you do whatever it is you have to do right here in Nazareth?"

"No, Mother," Jesus replied as gently as he could. "It cannot be. I must go where my Father leads me. I must do what he asks. And now is the time to begin."

Jesus took her into his strong arms and embraced her, kissed her on each tear-drenched cheek, threw his robe around his shoulders, took up his walking stick, and left. She watched him walk down the rocky lane, very straight of back, and with a strong sense of purpose evident in his bearing. He did not look back. He was far down the road when she gasped and then ran after him.

"Jesus, Jesus! Stop! Wait! You didn't say. . ." But it was no use. He was too far down the road, and he couldn't hear her. She just watched as he walked farther and farther away from her toward—where?

Since that day Mary had seen little of her son, and the extra effort required to be with him at Passover seemed well worth it.

She had planned on their being together for this year's paschal observance as soon as she knew that Jesus would be in Jerusalem. It was her only reason for being here now. She was sure he would be too busy to have much time for her but was reasonably certain that he would observe Passover, and the yearning in her heart to be near him was very great.

She had had to persuade her son, James, that she should come. He hadn't wanted her to because he felt she might endanger her own life. There were so many undercurrents abroad in Jerusalem, and James was also aware that with the thousands of additional people roaming the city, the very atmosphere changed. Anything could happen. He feared for her safety. It scared her to think her eldest son faced that much danger. *But what about that day of his royal ride into Jerusalem*? Her thoughts tried a more positive direction. *Couldn't that mean James was wrong; that all my children's fears were for nothing*?

It was so difficult to sort out her thoughts—to concentrate on Jesus' enemies and the danger, or on his friends who loved him and would protect him. It seemed to her that no one who knew Jesus was indifferent to him. It was hard for her to accept such diverse opinion about her beloved son—criticism, hatred, condemnation on the one hand; acceptance, love, and royal devotion on the other. Even though she was his mother and could be expected to think thus, she knew he was a man of integrity who deserved nothing but love from anyone.

They approached Jerusalem. The great stone walls of that city were not far off. They stood in awe at the splendor of the beautiful temple built by Herod. No matter how often they had beheld that sight, the effect was always the same. The sun reflected brightly off the gleaming white marble of the hundreds of Corinthian columns surrounding the temple area. The gold adornment made their house of worship even more dazzling, and the terraced roof with its needles of gold, placed there to discourage the birds, caught the sun's rays and danced with them. It was a breathtaking sight.

The band of pilgrims quickened its step, so close now to journey's end. They came over the crest of the hill and through the Mount of Olives, down the stony thoroughfare into the Kidron Valley below the city. They walked a short distance along this divide until they came to the road leading up the hill into the city. By now the immense crowds numbered in the thousands. People from many nations surrounded them. They saw all manner of strange dress and heard languages strange to their ears. They had to reckon with donkeys, lambs, even camels as they walked the road.

Lazarus picked up their own frightened lamb for fear it would be trampled underfoot. The pushing and jostling of strangers in a crowd had now replaced the friendly camaraderie and the spontaneous bursts of song. Now all concentrated on the business at hand—finding the place for their feasts and getting to the temple for the sacrifice.

Lazarus had made arrangements with a friend, Elian the weaver, for accommodations for celebrating the feast and for the overnight stay. He lived fairly close to the temple area by the Ephraim Gate, which made it convenient for them. So they headed for Elian's house as soon as they had entered the city gate.

Elian's wife greeted them and showed them the way. Deborah took them around the house to the large building in which Elian kept his looms, then left them to their preparations. They were grateful for the effort that Elian and Deborah had made to secure their comfort in this makeshift home. They had pushed the looms against the wall as much as possible. Blankets had been hung along two of the walls, dividing these two areas from the larger part of the room. Mats had even been provided for them on which to sleep. The bedrolls they had brought along would provide extra comfort. And in the large open area they had arranged five low tables in the usual manner for feasts, which was in the form of a large U. The open end allowed ease of movement for those serving. Around the outside of the tables reclining couches had been arranged, since it was the custom to recline during a feast.

As soon as they had surveyed their accommodations, Martha sent the men to fetch the things from the donkeys while she thought about how they should get organized for the feast. Maria took it upon herself to make Sara comfortable so she could rest. When the men brought in the baskets, Mary and Martha emptied them, setting everything to one side until they would return from the temple much later. It had been decided that Rebekah and the two younger children would stay behind with Sara while the others went to the temple. Rebekah put the two young ones down for a nap, grateful that they would be able to stay up late without becoming cranky.

It was only a short walk, so it was not long before they had passed through one of the gates into the temple area and crossed the esplanade into the Court of the Gentiles. With some difficulty, because of the crowding, they eventually made their way through the portal into the Court of the Women. Looking up to the lintel over the entrance, Mary saw once again the familiar golden vine entwined there, the symbol of Israel. Mary, Martha, and Maria could not go beyond this point, and so they waited and prayed while Lazarus, Simon, Matthias, and young Simon went into the Court of Israel. The women watched as the men then moved into the Court of the Priests, along with a multitude of other men bearing their sacrificial victims. When that court was filled, twenty men closed the heavy, gold-paneled bronze gate. The women then heard the shofar signaling the beginning of the sacrifice with three blasts—one long one followed by a quavering sound, then another long sustained blast. After that Mary could only visualize what was happening within, aided by the recounting of the sacrifice by Joseph many years before.

The priests held in their hands gold and silver basins that had no bases so they wouldn't be tempted to set them down. They stood in alternating rows, the gold and silver basins not mixed together. She knew that when Lazarus had slaughtered his lamb, the first priest caught the blood in his basin then passed it on to the next priest, exchanging his full basin for the empty one. And so it would go from priest to priest until it finally reached the priest closest to the altar. When he received the basin of blood, he dashed the blood against the base of the altar. Then after Lazarus had flayed the animal and cut it open, he removed the sacrificial portions of the entrails. After placing them on a tray, he gave them to a priest to burn at the altar. She could hear the Levites as they sang the Hallel continuously until all animals in the court had been sacrificed. Occasionally all of this would be punctuated by blasts of the shofar.

Mary lost count of how many times the Levites had sung the Hallel before the gate was opened and the first group of Israelites came out. The second group of men who had been waiting in the Court of Israel then entered the Court of the Priests. There would be three groups in all. It took a long time for all three groups to complete the ritual.

When the three women and the three men and young Simon finally found each other again afterwards, they were anxious to be on their way back to the others. The smell in the temple area nearly overpowered them. The strong incense that constantly burned could not absorb all of the smell. Mary hoped that their quarters were far enough away so that the acrid odor of burning entrails would not pursue them there.

When they returned to their temporary home, they found Sara up and feeling rested. Though they could not begin roasting the lamb until after sundown, Lazarus went outside to prepare the spit made of pomegranate wood.

The women busied themselves with preparing the feast. Mary gave her full energy to this task. Taking three napkins, she placed three thick unleavened cakes in each one and carefully wrapped them. She then fixed several plates with the prescribed food so that each person would have ready access to everything. On each plate she placed some of the charosheth they had made that morning, some horseradish, dandelion leaves, and a small bowl of salt water. As she did this, she thought about the meaning with which these things were imbued. All her life the symbolism representing this most important bit of Hebrew history had been repeated every year and had become so deeply ingrained in her that she would never forget any of it. It always made her feel special that God had loved the Hebrew nation so much that he had brought them out of their Egyptian slavery under very difficult circumstances. All the parts of the feast reminded them of these historical facts.

Her ancestors had eaten unleavened bread because there was no time to wait for the leavening action to work. They had to be ready to go at a moment's notice. The charosheth reminded them of the clay the Israelites had used in making bricks for the Egyptians. The cinnamon sticks in it looked like the straw used in the clay. The roasted egg that she added to each plate was in memory of the freewill offering of the feast. The horseradish, a bitter herb, reminded them of the harshness of slavery, and the leaves of the dandelion symbolized the branch of hyssop used to smear blood on the door lintels. The salt water had double meaning. It reminded them of the tears shed by the Hebrew slaves in Egypt and of the safe crossing of the Red Sea. And, of course, there was the lamb, symbolized by the roasted shank bone she would later place on a silver platter and put on the table. This reminded them of the lamb whose blood had been splashed on the doorposts and lintels to keep away the angel of death that had killed all firstborn males of the Egyptians.

It was an awesome thing to remember the lengths to which Moses and Aaron, with God leading them, had gone to rescue the Hebrew people from bondage and to build them into a strong nation. It had not been easy for them even after leaving Egypt, for they had wandered in the desert for forty long, tiresome years. But God took that opportunity to give them the Ten Commandments and all the other laws, and to teach them to live in dependence on him. And now, all these centuries later, they still killed lambs for the Passover—lambs that gave their lives for Israel's children—sacrificial lambs.

"Here are the wine cups." Martha broke Mary's chain of thought. "And I have also filled Elijah's cup. Everything else is arranged, I think. We can eat as soon as the lamb has been roasted."

Chapter Eight

Passover

"Blessed art Thou, O Eternal, Our God, King of the universe, Creator of the fruit of the vine. Blessed art Thou Lord, Our God, King of the universe, Who has brought us out from under the burdens of the Egyptians and delivered us from their bondage."

With this time-honored prayer Lazarus solemnly began the Passover ritual. He then took the Cup of Kiddush, which had already been poured, and drank it all.

When the others had all drunk their wine, Lazarus ceremonially washed his hands. Using special ceremonial water that had been kept in a large stone jar specifically for this purpose, he poured the water over his hands three times, fingertips held up so that the water ran down over his wrists. Having done this, he rubbed each hand with the fist of the other, then again poured water over his hands, this time with his fingers down and pouring from the wrists. With ceremonially clean hands, Lazarus took some of the dandelion greens, dipped them into the salt water, then prayed, "Blessed art Thou, O Eternal, Our God, King of the universe, Creator of the fruits of the earth." After eating some of the greens, Lazarus bade his guests to do the same.

Maria then rose from her place and poured a second cup of wine for everyone. As soon as she had returned to her place, six-year-old James, the youngest member of this gathering, spoke up. By tradition the youngest person present asked the necessary questions.

"Wherefore is this night different from all other nights? Any other night we may eat either unleavened or leavened bread, but on this night only unleavened bread; all other nights we may eat any species of herbs, but this night only bitter herbs; all other nights we do not even dip once, but this night we dip twice; all other nights we eat sitting or reclining, but this night we all recline."

As James sat down, he was regaled with the proud glances and happy smiles of his indulgent family, for this had been a pretty good speech for so young a lad. Mary smiled too as she remembered each of her boys when they had taken that same part in the ritual and how proud she had been of them.

Lazarus replied, "By strength of hand the Lord brought us out of Egypt, from the house of bondage. For when Pharaoh stubbornly refused to let us go, the Lord slew all the firstborn of man and the firstborn of cattle. When Pharaoh let the people go, God led them by the wilderness toward the Red Sea. And the Lord went before them by day in a pillar of cloud to lead them along the way, and by night in a pillar of fire to give them light, that they might travel by day and by night. When Pharaoh's armies pursued them, the Lord opened up a way through the Red Sea so that our people walked through the sea on dry land. Thus the Lord saved Israel that day from the hand of the Egyptians."

Lazarus concluded his story of the escape from Egypt on a high note of excitement, which was contagious. No sooner had he stopped speaking and bowed his head than the entire group burst out in joyous song, the first part of the Hallel:

> Praise the Lord! Praise, O servants of the Lord, praise the name of the Lord! Blessed be the name of the Lord from this time forth and for evermore! From the rising of the sun to its setting the name of the Lord is to be praised! The Lord is high above all nations, and his glory above the heavens!
>
> Who is like the Lord our God, who is seated on high, Who looks far down upon the heavens and the earth? He raises the poor from the dust, and lifts the needy from the ash heap, to make them sit with princes, with the princes of his people. He gives the barren woman a home, making her the joyous mother of children. Praise the Lord!
>
> When Israel went forth from Egypt, the house of Jacob from a people of strange language, Judah became his sanctuary, Israel his dominion.
>
> The sea looked and fled, Jordan turned back. The mountains skipped like rams, the hills like lambs. What ails you, O sea, that you flee? O Jordan, that you turn back? O mountains, that you skip like rams? O hills, like lambs? Tremble, O earth, at the presence of the Lord, at the presence of the God of Jacob, Who turns the rock into a pool of water, the flint into a spring of water.

As the voices faded away, Lazarus continued, "Originally our ancestors were idolaters, and Terah, the father of Abraham and Nahor, worshiped other gods. But Scripture says, 'I your God took your father Abraham and led him to Canaan, and multiplied his seed, and gave him Isaac; and I gave unto Isaac, Jacob and Esau… but Jacob and his children went down into Egypt.' Blessed be He Who kept His promises to Israel as it is said: 'And He said unto Abraham, "Know of a certainty that thy seed shall be strangers in a land that is not theirs, and shall serve them for four hundred years… and I shall judge that nation, and afterwards thy seed shall go forth with great abundance.'""

Lazarus raised his cup and said, "And it is that promise which has been the support of our ancestors, and ourselves, for not only one has risen up against us, but in every generation some have arisen against us to annihilate us, but the Most Holy, blessed be He, always delivers us out of their hands." He set down the chalice and continued, "With only a few persons… three score and ten souls, thy ancestors went down into Egypt because there was a famine in Canaan, and now God has made a great multitude, like stars in the heavens! And you became a nation, and the children of Israel were distinguished even in Egypt! You became exceedingly mighty, and the land was filled with Israelites. And the Egyptians became frightened of our great numbers! They decided to deal with us by putting us into bondage, lest we should side with their enemies. They placed taskmasters over us and laid heavy burdens of much building and many hard labors upon us. And we cried out to God, and God heard our groaning and remembered His covenant with Abraham, our father. And God saw our affliction, the separation from our wives and the murder of our male children.

"And God raised up Moses for our leader. And the pharaoh would not listen to Moses, so God sent many plagues, until the time that the pharaoh would believe that the holy and mighty God of the Israelites was mightier than any pharaoh, and the King of the universe. He sent frogs, vermin, and flies; the waters were turned to blood; He sent hail, locusts, boils, murrain, and the pharaoh would not release the children of Israel. So God Himself passed over and smote every firstborn of Egypt. And the pharaoh was frightened and cried out for us to leave the land of Egypt. But as we were leaving, he changed his mind and sent his armies after us. So God split the Red Sea for us and smote the Egyptians.

"Blessed art Thou, O God, King of the universe, Who has redeemed us and brought us to this night to eat unleavened bread and bitter herbs, that we may eat of the sacrifice of the Holy Paschal Lamb whose blood shall be for the acceptance and the redemption of our souls, Who has redeemed Israel. Blessed art Thou, O Lord our God, King of the universe, Who created the fruit of the vine." Everyone drank the Haggaddeh cup, a toast as it were to the proclaiming of God's great acts. After the wine was drunk, they all washed their hands in the same manner that Lazarus had done earlier. As they did so they chanted, "Blessed art Thou Who has sanctified us by Thy commandments and commanded us to wash our hands."

Choosing the center cake from the napkin before him, Lazarus prayed, "Blessed art Thou, O God, King of the universe, Who brings forth bread from the earth and Who has sanctified us by Thy commandments and commanded us to eat unleavened bread." Then he broke the bread into small pieces and passed it around to all, saying, "This is the bread of affliction which our forefathers ate in the land of Egypt. Whosoever is hungry, let him come and eat. Whosoever is in need, let him come and keep the Passover with us." He ate a small piece of the bread in his hand to remind them all that when they were slaves in Egypt, they never had a whole loaf of bread but only crusts.

Then taking some of the horseradish and placing it between two pieces of unleavened bread, he dipped it into the charosheth. The others followed his lead. As she ate the sop, as this "sandwich" was called, Mary thought of the slavery her ancestors had suffered and the blood bricks they had been forced to make for another of Israel's many oppressors.

As soon as they had all eaten of the sop, Martha and Maria brought the lamb to the table. Very efficiently they distributed the large platters of deliciously aromatic lamb. The atmosphere of the room changed from one of solemnity and worship, and even sleepiness on the part of some, to one of gaiety and friendly chatter. The children had become restive through the long ritual, especially little James. When their father, Matthias, allowed them to leave the table to release some of their pent-up energy, James came over to Mary and cuddled up to her, but only for a moment because he had been required to be still for too long.

Again Mary felt lonesome for her own grandchildren, longing to be with them for this occasion. Even though in Nazareth they could not feast on lamb because they were outside the bounds of Jerusalem, it was still a time of festivity and remembering, and a family time. Added to this was her bitter disappointment about Jesus' absence from her tonight. She again felt herself becoming very gloomy. She should have listened to James. Though she had not felt that she was in any personal danger, she had certainly heard enough to depress her spirit. She felt very much at odds with all the laughter and chatter going on around her and was disinclined to join in. But reminding herself once more that even one gloomy person could spoil the festivities for everyone else, she forced herself to enter into the gaiety.

All the seriousness of the past days seemed to have been forgotten on this night of remembrance. With Lazarus as their leader they had all remembered things of a faraway time and a faraway place, things that very definitely had an effect on all of their lives. It was their obligation to remember as though they themselves had experienced these things, even though it all happened far beyond the beginnings of their own experience. But now, in the relaxation of sharing a meal, they remembered things within their own lives, especially other Passover feasts.

"I'll never forget the year I knocked over my wine chalice as I reached for it to raise it for the blessing," Simon said. "And when Sara tried to help me, her sleeve dipped into a dish of charosheth. She pulled back so quickly that she upset her chalice. Everyone tried so hard to remain serious. Then Sara added further to the confusion. She brought more wine to refill my chalice, but as she started pouring, she completely missed the chalice. After that we could not hold back the laughter. So we all just let go for a few minutes. I had a hard time getting serious enough to start singing the second part of the Hallel, but we finally quieted down, and things returned to normal before it was finished."

By the time Simon had finished relating his tale, everyone was laughing heartily at the vision this invoked. How embarrassing for those involved, for this was a serious occasion, but how wonderful it was to be able to laugh about it now, and then too, for that matter.

Matthias, still laughing, said, "I remember that so well, Father, because that was a night for mistakes. Remember how I forgot the questions? After the first sentence my mind went completely blank, and it was only with your prompting that I was able to finish."

They ate the meal in this relaxed atmosphere, and Mary found herself relaxing too. By the time they all had eaten their fill, the whole lamb had been consumed. They would not have to destroy the leftovers as required, though in two days they must burn the bones and all other inedible parts. Again they all participated in the ceremonial washing of their hands, after which they finished eating the remaining unleavened bread. Martha placed the chalice she had filled earlier on a table near the door, which had been left slightly ajar for Elijah.

Lazarus then continued with the ritual words, "Gentlemen, let us pray."

In unison the men prayed, "Let us bless Him of Whose gifts we have partaken. Blessed art Thou, O Lord, King of the universe, Who created the fruit of the vine."

Together all eleven of them drank the Cup of Thanksgiving, then prayed together, "Blessed art Thou, O Lord, Our God, King of the universe, Who has created the fruit of the vine."

They resumed the singing of the Hallel.

> Not to us, O Lord, not to us, but to thy name give glory, for the sake of thy steadfast love and thy faithfulness!...
>
> The Lord has been mindful of us; he will bless us; he will bless the house of Israel; he will bless the house of Aaron; he will bless those who fear the Lord, both small and great. . .
>
> Praise the Lord, all nations! Extol him, all peoples! For great is his steadfast love toward us; and the faithfulness of the Lord endures forever. Praise the Lord!
>
> O give thanks to the Lord, for he is good; for his steadfast love endures forever!...
>
> This is the day which the Lord has made; let us rejoice and be glad in it. Save us, we beseech thee, O Lord! O Lord, we beseech thee, give us success!
>
> Blessed be he who enters in the name of the Lord! We bless you from the house of the Lord. The Lord is God, and he has given us light. Bind the festal procession with branches, up to the horns of the altar! Thou art my God, and I will give thanks to thee; thou art my God, I will extol thee.
>
> O give thanks to the Lord, for he is good; for his steadfast love endures forever!

After singing these words of praise and thanksgiving, the celebrants drank the fourth cup of wine, then sang the Great Hallel, from Psalm 136, a song of praise. They began:

> O give thanks to the Lord, for he is good, for his steadfast love endures forever.

As they repeated the litany, Mary thought on these familiar words so reverently spoken, each repetition of the phrase, "for his steadfast love endures forever," expressed with deepening intensity of feeling on the part of these faithful children of God. No wonder this was called the Great Hallel, for it showed the greatness of their God as he revealed himself from before the beginning, through the ages of time and creation, and down through their own eventful history. First came the elementary statement that God is God. Next they acknowledged that this great God is also Creator; he made the earth and the seas and the heavens with all of their lights both large and small. And from the time of their sojourn through history until now, he has been their avenger, Savior, sustainer, conqueror, and provider. As the final "for his steadfast love endures forever" filled the room with the air of joy and thanksgiving, Mary knew in her heart that this was true, for the God of the Israelites was indeed God of love.

When their voices had ceased ringing throughout the room, they then joined together in prayer, "All Thy works shall praise Thee, O Lord, our God. And Thy saints, the righteous, who do Thy good pleasure, and all Thy people, the house of Israel, with joyous song, let them praise and bless and sanctify and scribe the kingdom to Thy name, for from everlasting unto everlasting Thou art God."

Yet again they lifted their voices in prayer, "The breath of all that lives shall praise Thy name, O Lord, our God. And the spirit of all flesh shall continually glorify and exalt Thy memorial, O God, our King. For from everlasting unto everlasting Thou art God, and beside Thee we have no King, Redeemer, or Savior."

CHAPTER NINE

Surrender

When Jesus had sent Peter and John to Jerusalem to prepare the Passover, he and the others, restless but not wanting to return to the frenetic city just yet, left the peace of their spacious Bethany haven and walked toward Lazarus' large olive grove. Sporadic white clouds of almond blossoms gave off a sweet fragrance and contrasted sharply with the dark green of the olive leaves. They found an open area within the grove and sprawled on the ground beneath an almond tree. It was almost as though they knew this was to be their last time together in peace. Jesus seemed pensive. Not wanting to impose themselves on his solitude, they conversed quietly in groups of two and three.

"What do you suppose Jesus has on his mind this morning?" Philip asked Andrew. "Do you think he is worried about going back to Jerusalem?"

"I wouldn't doubt that. He knew the danger even before we came from Jericho last week. It's a miracle that something hasn't happened before this. I'm not too eager to go back there myself."

"I know what you mean, Andrew. We are in danger too as disciples of a wanted man. But that doesn't bother me nearly as much as that something should happen to him. What would we do without Jesus?"

"I don't know either how we could go on without him," Andrew said. "Even though he has taught us well how to go about the work he has been doing, it seems that all of our energy comes from him."

Andrew had not taken his worried gaze from Jesus' desolate form since they had settled themselves in this spot, and he continued to regard him in bewildered sadness. He remembered the excitement and anticipation he had felt when he first met Jesus three years ago. Now all that was replaced by despondency and confusion. *What will be the outcome of all that's happened this week*? he wondered.

"And Judas, look at him." Philip directed Andrew's reluctant gaze to the other lone figure amongst them. It was hard to know what Judas might be thinking, but his thick, dark eyebrows almost met over his nose, so deep was his scowl. He lay on his back, eyes closed, tension very much in evidence not only on his forehead but also in the set of his mouth and the rigidity of his body.

Andrew sighed. "Judas is a misfit. It seems he is no longer one with us. He disagrees too readily with so much that we say. Even though he shares little these days, his manner shows that he is very much discontented. If he would talk to us, perhaps we could help him find an answer to whatever is his problem."

"Perhaps, but I doubt he could be persuaded to more positive reasoning. He holds on to his grudges so doggedly; it's almost as though he's afraid someone will talk him out of them."

"You could be right. It seems to be much more than just a matter of disagreement; it's something deeper, darker, even sinister. That recent fiery outburst seems to be only a part of some greater turmoil. If it ever all spills out, I fear for us all."

Philip nodded. "I think you have a point, Andrew. I doubt that Judas can continue in our ministry in his present state. I wonder what will become of him."

"That's something I have thought about too. It's distressing, really, what has happened to Judas. I can't remember when I first noticed him changing; it was such a gradual thing. He used to be as enthusiastic as we were, but he has become so belligerent and seems to want no part of our company or our work anymore. As I look back, I can think of things he has said over the past year or so that I thought nothing of at the time, but which now I think marked the beginnings of the change."

"It's strange that he should be so unhappy. We have all changed and, except for Judas, for the better; at least I hope we have. I certainly feel that I have learned a lot from the Master. The rest of us have become different persons than we were three years ago—except for Judas. He alone has turned his back. Why? And what will be the result?"

The questions were unanswerable. They both knew that.

Andrew broke the silence that had followed their unhappy conversation. "We can only hope that in time Jesus will somehow win him back."

If these men had known what had really happened with Judas, and what they were all about to face within the next two days, beginning that very night, they would have been astounded.

The group had been in the grove for several hours. They spent most of the time engaged in quiet conversation, except for Jesus and Judas. Sometimes one or another of the group dozed off, tired from the strenuous days and their early morning rising that day. But when the sun was well past its zenith, they became restless and hungry. Jesus noticed the sounds of restlessness and roused himself from his reverie to suggest they be on their way. "Peter and John will be ready for us soon."

With a curious mixture of relief and reluctance they picked themselves up off the ground to head for Jerusalem. They walked through the village and on to the main road, joining the other pilgrims who were singing their way to the city and celebration.

Having arrived at Josiah's house, they immediately went to the upper room where they found Peter and John still setting out plates of bread and urns of watered wine. Everything had been prepared according to Jesus' instructions for the celebration that they hoped would revive all their spirits. There was no Passover lamb, a fact that caused no small amount of wonder among the disciples as they saw what had been provided for their celebration. It wouldn't be the first time they had observed Passover without lamb, but being within the walls of Jerusalem this year, they had expected it. Well, Jesus must have a reason, and they would soon discover it.

At sunset they came together round the table. If they had hoped that this would be a jubilant, or at least happier, evening, Jesus' opening words destroyed that hope.

"I have earnestly desired to eat this Passover with you before I suffer, for I shall not eat it again until it is fulfilled in the kingdom of God." Again the disciples were discomfited. Again he talked as though he were about to leave them.

Without further comment they began the traditional ritual of the Passover observance. At the very point where the head of the house was to take the bread, break it, and serve it, however, Jesus departed from tradition. Instead of saying, "This is the bread of affliction which our forefathers ate in the land of Egypt," he said, "Take and eat; this is my body." Wondering at the change of symbolism that Jesus placed upon the bread, they silently ate.

When they had eaten, he picked up the silver cup in front of him and said, "Drink of it, all of you; for this is my blood of the covenant, which is poured out for many for the forgiveness of sins. I tell you I shall not drink again of this fruit of the vine until that day when I drink it new with you in my Father's kingdom." Slowly each took the cup and sipped from it, beginning with John at Jesus' right hand, then Peter, and Andrew and on around until at last it came to Judas and was emptied. Not one allowed his eyes to wander from Jesus during the entire time, knowing that something momentous was happening. No one wanted to miss a single word or action. The intimacy of their relationship was never more deeply felt than in this hour. They knew that Jesus had shared something precious with them and they felt privileged to be included. At this point they possessed no understanding of recent events or of this evening's mystery. They could only trust that in time Jesus would help them out of this darkness and back into the light, and then they would know the true meaning of all they were experiencing.

When Jesus took the cup from Judas, he carefully set it on the table in front of himself. In an emotionally husky voice he said, "I say to you, one of you will betray me."

A gasp echoed around the room, from all as one. If anyone had glanced at Judas at that moment, the startled look that accompanied his audible surprise could not have been missed. Immediately the room became alive with one voice after another questioning in unbelieving consternation, "Is it I, Lord?" "Is it I?" Peter leaned over to John and said, "Tell us who it is of whom he speaks."

So John asked Jesus, "Lord, who is it?"

"He who has dipped his hand in the dish with me will betray me. The Son of man goes to his death as it is written of him, but woe to that man by whom the Son of man is betrayed! It would have been better for him if he had not been born." Jesus spoke sadly, for he loved Judas in spite of his treachery.

Judas, in a voice hardly above a whisper, asked, "Is it I, Master?"

Jesus responded in an equally muted voice, "You have said so. What you are going to do, do quickly."

Immediately Judas left the room. As he turned his back on three years of hope and happiness, he wondered how Jesus knew that he had betrayed him. He felt as though all those men he had just left condemned him, and he felt very uncomfortable. Glad when he reached the street, Judas went to alert the chief priests that the time had come. Relief that this whole matter was about to come to a conclusion flooded him. He hurried toward his chosen destiny.

Judas' idea that the others had condemned him, however, existed only in his own mind. On the contrary, even after what Jesus had just said to John, Judas' leaving had puzzled them.

"Perhaps," Nathanael whispered to Philip, "he has gone to give an offering for the poor at the temple."

As the sound of Judas' sandals faded down the stairs, the disciples discussed among themselves the possible leadership positions each would hold as their ministry with Jesus took on greater dimensions. What began as quiet speculation soon erupted into a full-fledged dispute.

Matthew had begun the discussion. "Now that Judas has gone, I'll say what has been much on my mind lately. We have seen how he has changed. He is sullen and secretive, and I for one think he should no longer carry our money pouch. I'm not sure I trust him anymore."

"It's true," agreed Simon Zealotus. "He keeps to himself, and he leaves us to go places of which we have no knowledge. When he comes back, he offers no explanation."

"We have all seen this change," Matthew spoke for the rest. "I think it would be a good idea if we appointed a new treasurer, and I think it only fitting that I be given the responsibility since I am no stranger to the keeping of monies."

"Why you, my brother?" queried James, Matthew's brother. "I too was once a tax-gatherer and am well able to keep the treasury."

"But I am your elder and therefore the one to whom the responsibility should fall."

"Your age makes you more important than I?" countered James.

The brothers were once again in competition, a frequent thing in the past, but something that had become less of a problem since they had come under the influence of the Master.

"Well, if it's to be a matter of who is most important here, then I would say it was John or me," suggested James, son of Zebedee. "After all, we are cousins of the Master. Or it could even be Peter. Jesus has frequently chosen us three to share in his private times."

John agreed and added his own argument to substantiate the claim of his brother, James. "We have perhaps given up more to follow. We didn't need to live in poverty; our father is wealthy. We would have inherited a lucrative business. We owned two houses and had hired servants at our beck and call. We could still be living in luxury had we not chosen to accept the hardship of empty purses for the privilege of being with the Master."

"I was first called," Andrew joined in. "Maybe that makes me more important than all of you, but I have no desire for such a distinction."

"Nor I," Philip stated. "Isn't it enough that we are privileged to learn from the Master, whom we know to be the Messiah? What else could be more important?"

"It is a privilege that only twelve of us in all of Judea and Galilee have had. And that would be enough, but how are we to determine how to delegate responsibility without some method of determining importance?" Matthew was truly puzzled.

"You would know who is greatest among you?" Jesus wearily but patiently asked them. *Has nothing I've told them made any impact at all? How can I leave them, as unprepared for continuing my ministry as they are? Three years I've taught them the role of a servant, yet here they still argue over position. They carry on as though nothing has changed in these last days.*

"The kings of the Gentiles exercise lordship over them; and those in authority over them are called benefactors. But not so with you; rather let the greatest among you become as the youngest, and the leader as the one who serves. True greatness is achieved only through service to others. For which is the greater, one who sits at table, or one who serves? Is it not the one who sits at table? But I am among you as one who serves. You are all privileged, and important, for you have assisted me in my service to others. You are those who have continued with me even in my trials. As you have shared my trials, you will also share my joy. You will sit on thrones and judge the twelve tribes of Israel according to whether they have accepted or rejected the proclaimed word of the Father."

Jesus rose from the table, laid aside his outer robe, and fastened a towel to his tunic in the manner of a slave. Then he poured water into the ewer and crouched at the feet of Nathanael. Embarrassed that Jesus had so degraded himself before them all, he made as if to withdraw his feet. But at Jesus' insistent look, he refrained from doing so. Jesus poured the water over his feet, gently drying them with the towel. In this manner he continued around the table. When he came to Simon Peter, Peter protested, withdrawing his feet.

"Lord do *you* wash *my* feet?"

Jesus answered, "What I am doing you do not know now, but afterward you will understand."

Peter replied, "You shall never wash my feet. *Never!*"

"If I do not wash you, you have no part in me or in my work."

In his usual impulsive manner Peter responded, "Lord, not my feet only but also my hands and my head!"

"Peter, Peter. He who has bathed already does not need to wash, except for his feet, for he is clean all over. You are already clean, but not all of you." Symbolically all of the disciples were clean, that is, not contaminated by the evil one, except Judas, but the disciples did not understand the meaning of "but not all of you."

Jesus washed Peter's feet, then continued on to John, and then the rest of the way around the table until he had washed the feet of all eleven men. Except for the conversation between Jesus and Peter, the men relished a quiet time of awed contemplation. The washing of people's feet was for servants; Jesus was their Master. It required serious consideration and a drastic departure from cultural prejudice.

When he had finished, he put on his discarded robe and resumed his place at the table. He studied them for a moment, understanding their puzzlement, then said, "Do you know what I have done to you? You call me Teacher and Lord, and you are right, for so I am." Jesus acknowledged the dignity of his office even though he had just performed a slave's task. "If I then, your Lord and Teacher, have washed your feet, you also ought to wash one another's feet. For I have given you an example, that you also should do as I have done to you." It is never beneath the dignity of anyone to serve another, even in the most menial of tasks. If Jesus could do such things without losing dignity, so too can his disciples.

"Truly, I say to you, a servant is not greater than his master; nor is he who is sent greater than he who sends him. If you understand the things I am teaching you, then blessed are you if you do them. You are not all obedient; one has chosen another course in order that the Scripture may be fulfilled, 'He who ate my bread has treated me brutally.'" In sharing a meal with the Master, Judas outwardly offered his loyalty though he knew he was not loyal. This had made his deed all the more terrible. "I tell you this now, before it takes place, so that when the treachery does take place, you will have been forewarned and may believe that I am he."

Troubled in spirit, his voice sorrowful, he continued.

"Little children, only a little while longer I am going to be with you. You will look for me, but you cannot come with me. A new commandment I give to you, that you love one another; even as I have loved you, you also must love one another. By this all men will know that you are my disciples."

"Where are you going, Lord?" Simon Peter wanted to know.

"Where I am going you cannot follow me now; but at a later time you shall follow after me."

Not satisfied, Peter persisted, "Lord, why can't I follow you now? I will lay down my life for you."

"Will you lay down your life for me?" Jesus asked him. "You will all fall away, for it is written, 'I will strike the shepherd, and the sheep will be scattered.' But after I am raised up, I will go before you to Galilee."

"Even though they all fall away, I will not," Peter declared.

"Peter, Peter. Satan has demanded to have you, but I have prayed for you that your faith may not fail; and when you have repented of your loss of faith, you will strengthen your brothers."

"Lord, I would go to prison for you, even die for you!" Peter strongly insisted.

Jesus said, "I tell you, Peter, the cock will not crow this day before you deny three times that you know me."

"No, Lord! It cannot be! I will never deny you. If I must die with you, I will not deny you."

All the disciples echoed his impassioned words.

Then Jesus said to them, "When I sent you out with no purse or bag or sandals, did you lack anything?"

"No, Lord. Nothing."

"But now, let him who has a purse take it, and likewise a bag. And let him who has no sword sell his mantle and buy one. These things were unnecessary before, but now you must go into a world more dangerous than before. Do not be forceful, only wary."

Simon Zealotus said, "Look, here are two swords."

Jesus nodded sadly, "It is enough."

For several moments he sat silently and then whispered, "There is so much to tell you, and so little time." He paused before continuing. "Don't trouble yourselves with the things that fret the soul. As you have trusted God, trust me. I am going to prepare a place for you with my Father, so that when you come we may be together."

"But Lord," Thomas said, "we do not know where you are going. How can we know the way?"

Jesus said to him, "I am the Way and the Truth and the Life. It is through me that you come to the Father."

Philip spoke up. "Lord, show us the Father and we shall be satisfied."

"Philip, Philip, have I been with you so long and yet you do not know me? The sheep know their shepherd, but you do not know me. You have seen me, and whoever has seen me has seen the Father. The words I speak are the words of the Father. I am in the Father and the Father is in me. After all this time with me do you not yet understand this? We are one, the Father and I. Believe me when I tell you this. I tell you also that whoever believes in me shall do the things that I have done, and greater things even than that. Whatever you ask in prayer, in my name, I will do it.

"I have said to you that you should love one another as I have loved you. Greater love has no man than this, that a man lay down his life for his friends.

"You heard me say, 'I go away, and I will come to you.' If you loved me, you would have rejoiced, because I go to my Father.

A little while, and you will see me no more; again a little while, and you will see me."

Philip turned aside to Nathanael and said, "What is this that he says to us, 'A little while and you will not see me, and again a little while, and you will see me,' and 'because I go to my Father?'"

"The world will see me no more, but you will," Jesus told them. "I will return to you."

Jude said, "Lord, how will you show yourself to us but not to the world?"

Jesus answered, "True disciples are obedient. If you love me, keep my commandments, for by so doing you show your love for me. Whoever loves me will keep my word and obey my commandments, and I will make myself known to that person. You are my friends if you do what I command you.

"The world, those who do not obey my commandments, will not know me.

"I have chosen you, and appointed you for the work of the kingdom. You are my witnesses because you have been with me since the beginning. I have shared my life and my thoughts with you for three years.

"Remember what I said to you, 'A servant is not greater than his master.' If the world hates you, know that it has hated me before it hated you, and because you are my disciples the world will hate you. If they persecuted me, they will persecute you; if they kept my word, they will keep yours also. They will put you out of the synagogues; indeed, there will come a time when whoever kills you will think he is offering service to God. There are those who will follow you, but many will oppose you.

"They will do all this because they have not known the Father, nor me. You will have great sorrow, but your sorrow will turn into joy. Joy comes out of pain. 'The Spirit of the Lord God is upon me, because the Lord has anointed me to grant to those who mourn in Zion the oil of gladness instead of mourning.'

You have sorrow now, but I will see you again and your hearts will rejoice, and no one will take your joy away from you. In the world you have tribulation, but be of good cheer, I have overcome the world.

"When I have gone, you will no longer be able to ask anything of me, but whatever you ask of the Father, he will give it to you in my name. You have never asked anything in my name; ask and you will receive and you will have complete joy.

"You will not be forsaken when I have gone from you. I have spoken to you of many things, teaching you while I have been here; but when I am gone the Father will give you a Counselor, the Holy Spirit that will dwell in you, and that will teach you all the things you need to know when you need to know them. It is by this Spirit that you will know me when I return. I will leave my peace with you, not outward peace that the world understands and that can be taken away, but my peace that is within you and that stays with you in spite of outward turmoil."

Andrew leaned toward Philip and whispered, "Would that Judas were here now. It might have helped him to know that Jesus would bring peace to his troubled mind."

Philip nodded agreement.

Jesus continued with his discourse. "I have told you all these things to keep you from falling away and so that when the time of their fulfillment comes, you may remember that I told you of them.

"I have spoken to you in figures; the time is coming when I shall no longer speak so but will tell you plainly of the Father. The Father himself loves you, because you have loved me and have believed that I came from the Father. I came from the Father and have come into the world; again, I am leaving the world and going to the Father."

Thomas spoke up, "Ah, now you are speaking plainly, not in any figure! Now we know that you know all things and need no one to question you; by this we believe that you came from God."

Jesus said, "Do you now believe? The hour is coming, indeed it has come, when you will be scattered every man to his home and will leave me alone; yet I am not alone for the Father is with me."

When Jesus had spoken these words, he lifted up his eyes to heaven and prayed, "Father, the hour has come; glorify the Son that the Son may glorify you, since you have given him power over all mankind, to give eternal life to all whom you have given him. And this is eternal life, that they know you, the only true God, and Jesus Christ whom you have sent. I glorified you on earth, having accomplished the work which you gave me to do; and now, Father, bring me again into the glory of your own presence, the glory which I had with you before the world was made.

"I have manifested your name to the men whom you gave me, and they have kept your word. They know that everything that you have given me is from you. I am praying for them. Keep them in your name which you have given me, that they may be one, even as we are one. While I was with them, I kept them, and none of them is lost but the son of perdition, fulfilling the Scripture. I do not pray that you should take them out of the world, but that you should protect them from the evil one. They are not of the world, even as I am not of the world. Sanctify them in the truth. For their sake I consecrate myself, that they also may be consecrated in truth.

"I do not pray for these only, but also for those who are to believe in me through their word, that they may all be united in spirit, so that the world may know that you have sent me and that you have loved the world even as you have loved me. Father, I desire that they also, whom you have given me, may be with me where I am, to behold my glory which you have given me in your love for me before the foundation of the world.

O righteous Father, the world has not known you, but I have known you, and these here with me now know that you have sent me. I made known to them your name, and I will make it known, that the love with which you have loved me may be in them, and that I may dwell in them."

When Jesus had finished encouraging them, and praying for them, he remained quiet, allowing them to absorb the impact of his words. He knew that full realization of what he meant would not be theirs until some future time. They would continue his ministry without him, in spite of persecution, when they knew from their own experience the power of the Holy Spirit, the Counselor who was to come.

After a time someone began softly humming a familiar hymn, and soon they all joined together in its singing, strongly, with considerable feeling. Having sung the hymn through, they left the upper room. Walking through the now quiet city, through the deserted Court of the Gentiles at the temple, they went out through the Sheep Gate, heading for the Mount of Olives.

If the city was quiet and the temple deserted, the Tower of Antonia was not. The Romans had strategically placed this symbol of foreign pagan intervention at the northwest corner of the temple area. The men felt the dominating, powerful occupation of their city as they silently passed by it. While devout Jews gathered within their homes at this dark, midnight hour, the soldiers lounged about outside the tower or roamed the streets of the area. Their coarse language and raucous laughter pierced the air. These soldiers had no war to fight and nothing to do with their off-duty time except to carouse. All self-respecting women remained in the protection of their homes. As Jesus and his companions passed by to the east, away from the tower, these crude and carousing soldiers did not even notice them.

When they came to the Mount of Olives, Jesus said to them, "Sit here while I pray, and you too pray that you may not enter into temptation."

Taking Peter, James, and John, he went a little farther away into the Garden of Gethsemane. Immediately he became visibly distressed and troubled. He said to them, "My soul is very sorrowful, even to death; remain here, and watch."

Going a little farther, he fell on the ground and prayed. "Abba, Father, all things are possible to you; remove this cup from me; yet not what I will, but what you will." For a long time he remained there, wrestling with the fear that assaulted his soul, tempting him to shun the pain of what lay ahead. Yet he desired to be obedient to the task given him by the Father, and so his distress was great.

Leaving the solitude of his struggle, he went back to the three he had left a little way off and found them sleeping. He said to Peter, "Simon, Simon, are you asleep? Could you not watch with me one hour? Watch and pray that you may not enter into temptation."

Peter blinked awake, but his eyelids were heavy and his mind too foggy to respond.

"The spirit indeed is willing," Jesus said gently and with understanding, "but the flesh is weak."

Again Jesus went away to struggle with the spiritual forces that opposed him. Again he prayed, "Father, if it is possible, let this hour pass from me." Overwhelmed by the agitation of his soul, he perspired profusely as he struggled to yield himself to the Father. After a time, he went to seek support from his three companions. He found them sleeping again. He said to them, "Such a short time it is. Could you not stay awake for this short time to comfort me in my sorrow?"

But their minds, lost in foggy clouds of sleep, could not think to answer him.

Jesus returned to his solitude, more distressed even than before. He knelt beside an immense boulder, not far from his sleepy friends, and cried to the Father. His agony surpassed the previous time of prayer so that he sweat huge drops of blood that fell to the ground. He prayed, "Father, if you are willing, remove this cup from me; nevertheless not my will, but yours, be done."

While he continued to kneel in silence, following his painful declaration of obedience, an angel appeared to him from heaven and strengthened him. He knew then that the Father had heard his plea. Though he could not alter the plan, whatever lay before him, God his Father would sustain him through it.

Coming again to the disciples, he said, "Are you still sleeping and taking your rest? Behold, the hour is at hand, and the Son of man is betrayed into the hands of sinners. Rise, let us be going; see, my betrayer is at hand." The disciples awoke at those words.

Before Jesus had finished speaking, Judas came leading a band of men with swords and clubs, and bearing torches in order to find their way in the dark olive grove. He knew this spot well and had been reasonably certain that Jesus would come here once he left the upper room. He led an armed force accompanied by officers of the chief priests and Pharisees, an unlikely combination of people. They pierced the utter quiet of their sanctuary with their clattering and chattering, and the blackness of the dark night with their smoking firebrands. The Blackness was not only about them, but also within. The invasion left the unwary disciples stunned.

Before coming to the garden, Judas had given the men a sign so that there would be no mistake in identifying the intended prisoner in the darkness. "Seize the man whom I shall kiss." So when Judas walked up to the Master, he said, "Hail, Master," and kissed him on the cheek.

Softly Jesus said to Judas, "Judas, would you betray the Son of man with a kiss?"

Then he moved forward and said to the chief captain, "Whom do you seek?"

He answered, "Jesus of Nazareth."

"I am he."

They all drew back and fell to the ground.

Again Jesus asked, "Whom do you seek?"

Again the chief captain replied, "Jesus of Nazareth."

"I told you that I am he; so, if you are looking for me, let these men go." He said that to fulfill the words he had spoken earlier, "Of those whom you gave me I lost not one." Then they came forward to take him.

Peter, true to his impetuous nature, pulled out his sword and slashed the air in wild anger and panic. He struck Malchus, the slave to the high priest, cutting off his right ear.

"No more of this!" admonished Jesus. "Peter, sheathe your sword, for all who take the sword will perish by the sword. Do you think that I cannot appeal to my Father, and he will at once send me more than twelve legions of angels? But if I did that, how would the Scriptures be fulfilled? What is happening must happen."

Turning to Malchus, he touched his ear and healed it. Then addressing his captors, he said, "Have you come out as against a robber, with swords and clubs to capture me? Day after day I sat in the temple teaching, and you did not seize me. But this is your hour; the power of darkness is yours. The night hides your deed in this lonely place."

Upon seeing their Master surrender, all the disciples without exception fled from the place. Had it been only a couple of hours ago that they pledged never to leave him—even to die with him?

CHAPTER TEN

Condemnation

Deserted by his closest friends, as he had said he would be, Jesus knew that they had escaped immediate danger. But what about his own situation? Soldiers had tied his hands behind him with rough leather thongs, an unnecessary precaution since he had willingly given himself over to the authorities and would not try to escape. This was not a consideration for them, of course. Unused to taking docile prisoners, they treated him as they treated all prisoners. A guard on each side grasped him by the upper arms, propelling him from his garden sanctuary down into the Kidron Valley where they followed its rift below the walls of the city.

The group hurriedly moved over the rough, rocky terrain of the valley rift. Jesus stumbled often because of the darkness, unable to watch his footing. The moon was not very bright, and the trees and other foliage cast deceiving shadows. The flickering of the torches caused things to appear that weren't there and hid the impediments that were. Far from the best way to return to the city, it was the most direct and presented the least danger of being seen. When they had come to the Gate of the Waters, they entered the Lower City and soon found themselves on the road leading to the palace of Caiaphas in the elite Upper City.

The high priest had gathered together certain members of the Sanhedrin. This was the administrative body of Jewish religious law, composed of seventy-one members taken from the ranks of the chief priests, scribes, and elders. As soon as the chief priests had come to him earlier that night with Judas' message, Caiaphas had sent messengers, calling together as many as possible. He wanted at least twenty-three present to ensure a quorum. These officials hadn't been happy about having to leave their homes so late at night, especially the night of a high holy day, but knowing that they had worked toward this moment for many weeks, they found their way to Caiaphas' home. Eventually the soldiers who arrested Jesus would bring him here.

But first they brought him to Annas.

Annas still retained a great deal of power. He spoke with the authority of one who expected immediate and unquestioning compliance. He had requested the opportunity to question Jesus personally. He had heard a variety of things about this man that had at first puzzled him and then angered him, the disturbance at the temple being a case in point. The claims to supernatural abilities that had been made on his behalf also piqued his curiosity. This did not concern him much since others had made supernatural claims before. None, however, had held the allegiance of the people for so long, nor had they exhibited their knowledge of Scripture so adroitly as he, nor even approached his mental acuity. What concerned him about Jesus was much more serious.

The Jews walked a thin line in their relationship with Rome. Emotions ran high when Israel's position as a nation was challenged in any way. The Jews believed themselves to be a theocratic nation, governed only by the laws of God. They were recalcitrant, difficult to hold in place, stirred easily to anger when their independent political-religious pursuits were denied—or threatened. For this reason Rome had allowed certain concessions to this province. Offensive military standards, bearing the likeness of the emperor and claims to his divinity, were permitted only in Caesarea, never in Jerusalem, the hotbed of unrest. The Sanhedrin, by appointment, had domestic power in all things and answered to the procurator who spent most of his time in Caesarea. The Sanhedrin saw that the people cooperated in maintaining Roman rule. Their position was justified only so long as they managed to keep the peace.

Now this upstart Nazarene had placed them all in jeopardy. His radical ideas would destroy them all. The more he thought on these things, the more angry Annas became. When the soldiers brought Jesus to him, he spat out in scornful wrath, "What is it that you and your disciples have been teaching that causes the people to want to make you king?"

Jesus answered, "I have spoken openly to the world; I have said nothing secretly. Why do you ask me? Ask those who have heard me, what I said to them; they can answer you."

Hardly had the words passed his lips than a sharp slap resounded, leaving the imprint of the perpetrator's hand on Jesus' cheek.

The guard who had struck him asked, "Is that how you answer the high priest?"

Jesus said, "If I have spoken wrongly, then show where I am wrong; but if I have spoken rightly, why do you strike me?"

Because he had no witnesses to testify that Jesus was wrong, and did not wish to consider that Jesus might be speaking the truth, Annas spoke sharply to the guards, "Take him to Caiaphas."

So they came to Caiaphas. He and others of the Sanhedrin, along with searched-out witnesses, had impatiently awaited their arrival.

Judas also waited there, having made his way directly to the appointed spot, knowing that whatever Annas wanted was unimportant. The significant action would occur here. He was anxious for proceedings to get under way. Ever since he bestowed that terrible kiss in the garden, his heart had grown heavy from playing this dangerous and hurtful game. As they had walked through the Kidron Valley at midnight, other walks in other places had come to mind—walks that led to ministry, walks that led to seclusion, walks that always included friendly camaraderie and serious discourse, walks that often found him by the Master's side, Jesus' arm across his shoulder, loving him, comforting him, encouraging him. What had seemed so right only hours ago began to feel very wrong.

Judas shrank back when Jesus was brought into the room. He did not want to face the hurt in Jesus' eyes if he should see him. In fact, he wished now he hadn't even come. According to Jewish court law, the accuser was the prosecutor. As the one who had delivered Jesus to them, Judas would have to witness, thus formally bringing charges. But somehow he no longer wanted to do that. He knew that the Sanhedrin would judge him guilty, for they had already reached the decision two nights earlier to find a way to kill him. He was no longer sure that this was the answer he wanted, or if it was ever really the answer he wanted.

Being such a strict believer in the law, Judas found himself considerably disturbed when he discovered the Sanhedrin had deviated from the law. Instead of acting as the jury, their only legal responsibility, they had already made the accusation, reached the verdict, and determined the punishment before the trial ever began. They simply needed to have the man brought before them for an outward show of a trial, leading to conviction and sentencing. He needn't have worried about the part he might be called upon to play in this farce. These men had already brought in witnesses they could rely on to give the "evidence" they wished to hear. Judas knew this violated the law requiring that witnesses must appear voluntarily and become the accusers. It was a good law because it helped to prevent the kind of thing that was about to happen to Jesus.

The council heard the testimony of several of these witnesses. Many came forward, but no two of them agreed on any point, and their testimony certainly could not command a death sentence.

Finally, two men came forward with the desired accusation. "This man said, 'I am able to destroy the temple of God and to build it in three days.'"

Caiaphas rose and said to Jesus, "Have you an answer to make? What is it that these men testify against you?"

But Jesus stood silent.

Caiaphas spoke again, heatedly. "You have made a threat against our temple. This is the same thing as threatening to destroy our religion. And the threat involves a claim to superhuman power. You would do in three days what it took hundreds of men twenty years to accomplish? I adjure you by the living God, tell us you are the Christ, the Son of God."

"I am, and you will see the Son of man sitting at the right hand of Power, and coming with the clouds of heaven."

Upon hearing those words, Caiaphas tore his cloak from end to end, the appropriate response to blasphemous words, and said, "He has uttered blasphemy. Why do we still need witnesses? You have now heard his blasphemy. What is your judgment?"

"He deserves death!" echoed through the room.

Caiaphas then turned to the guards and said, "Take him to the dungeon. We will bring him before the Sanhedrin at dawn, to inform them of the results of this hearing, to vote, and to pronounce sentence."

When the guards had taken him, they began to spit in his face and to strike him. "Prophesy to us, you Christ. Who is it that struck you?" Handling him in this rough manner, they left the room.

In the meantime Peter and John had come to the house of Caiaphas. They had not been able to desert Jesus totally. As they left the Mount of Olives, Peter had suggested that they watch and see where Jesus was taken. So they hid among the shadows until Judas' band passed them. Covertly, they followed at a good distance, never letting them out of their sight. When at last they came to the house of Caiaphas, Peter waited outside the door while John entered the courtyard and spoke to the maid who kept the door.

"This is my friend. I want to bring him into the courtyard while I see to business with Caiaphas."

Because she knew John as the son of Zebedee, a good friend of Caiaphas and a frequent visitor here, she agreed and allowed Peter into the courtyard.

As Peter passed by her, she said, "Are not you also one of this man's disciples?"

"I am not," he stated vehemently.

John went into the house and left Peter to sit with the guards around the charcoal fire they had kindled. Peter shivered, as much from the trauma of the night's experiences as from the cold that seeped into his bones. He felt miserable, frightened, and confused. He spread his hands toward the fire as though to gather its warmth to his cold body, staring into the mesmerizing, dancing flames. A wild jumble of thoughts flashed through his mind. A voice immediately beside him startled him, causing him to jump.

"Are you not also one of his disciples?" The guard closest to him spoke.

Swearing an oath, he denied it, "I am not!"

Agitated, he left the warmth of the fire and the inquisitiveness of the guards and paced the courtyard, wondering what was happening to Jesus, and what had happened to himself. Finally he came to the porch, hoping to catch some hint of the proceedings inside the house.

One of the high priest's servants stood by the step. Peter recognized him as having been in the garden at the time of the arrest, a relative of Malchus. Before he could slip away, the servant said, "Did I not see you in the garden with him?"

Again with an oath Peter denied it. "I do not know the man."

While he was still speaking the cock crowed, and Peter remembered what Jesus had said earlier that very night. "Before the cock crows, you will deny me three times." As Jesus was led along the porch, he turned and looked at Peter. Knowing what he had done, and knowing that Jesus had heard, was more than Peter could bear. He went away and wept bitterly.

With Jesus safely in the dungeon under the palace, Caiaphas wasted no time in sending for the remaining members of the Sanhedrin. He wanted the trial convened at the earliest possible moment, which was dawn. Dawn would come quickly since Jesus' arrest had occurred after midnight, and the time the hearing had taken left only about three hours to prepare for the trial.

As the sun's mauve rays gradually erased the gray from the pre-dawn sky, the elite members of the Sanhedrin began to arrive. The entire seventy-one had assembled and taken their accustomed places by the time the sun had risen above the horizon.

Dragging Jesus, who had had no food since the meal he shared with his disciples, nor any sleep since their last night in Bethany, the guards brought him before Caiaphas and the Sanhedrin.

When he stood before them, bedraggled and bound, Caiaphas again put the question to him. "Are you the Christ, the Son of God? If you are the Christ, tell us."

But he said to them, "If I tell you, you will not believe; and if I ask you, you will not answer. But from now on the Son of man shall be seated at the right hand of the power of God."

Someone asked again, "Are you the Son of God, then?"

"You say that I am."

One of their number shouted, "What further testimony do we need? We have heard it ourselves from his own lips."

"But we must put it to the vote," Jacob reminded them. "And let me remind you that for conviction involving a sentence of death, it is necessary to have a majority by at least two votes in favor. If we do not have that, then he must be acquitted."

"Yes," Caiaphas conceded. "We know that. It's the law."

Judas wondered why they acknowledged that law when so many others had been disregarded throughout the early morning hours. He had not left Caiaphas' house after the preliminary hearing. Having observed during those pre-dawn hours how the interrogation had taken place, he realized how eagerly they seized the opportunity to find Jesus worthy of death. Nothing the witnesses said interested them, since they did not agree, and inconsistent evidence could not be accepted. When they finally elicited what they considered to be an admission from Jesus that he was indeed the Son of God, the discussion ended. Jesus' own confession, if one could call it that, convicted him. They did not try to reason with him, to reprimand him, to warn him of the dangers of his chosen course, and to threaten punishment if he continued to persist in it, as they were required to do.

Whatever Judas had hoped would happen as a result of his turning Jesus over to the Sanhedrin was obviously not going to happen. Jesus did not call down the angels of heaven for his protection. He just stood, meekly accepting all that they did to him. Waiting through the remainder of the night for the convening of the Sanhedrin, Judas found himself hoping that the vote would not be adequate for a death sentence, or that it would be unanimous. Unanimous agreement would also free him since in such cases it was considered that the defendant had no one to speak for him. Death under such circumstances would not be legal. But Judas knew that Jesus had sympathizers on the Council who would not vote against him, so the best he could hope for was a wide margin of disagreement.

As the interrogation continued, Judas fully realized that ridding themselves of Jesus by execution was the only concern of the majority sitting on the Council, and they would go to any lengths to accomplish it. They perjured themselves, breaking one of the Ten Commandments of Moses. They even disregarded their own laws, one of which required that trials for capital offenses must be conducted during the daytime. If they condemned the prisoner to death, the trial was not to be concluded until the next day. During the intervening time the members of the court were to meet together to discuss the case, eating little and drinking no wine. Because of this two-day ruling, they could convene no trial on the day before the Sabbath. Yet here it was, the day before the Sabbath, and the trial was proceeding very much as the hearing had during the night.

Judas sat watching in abject misery, helpless now in the wake of the destruction he had helped to bring about. The time for the vote had come, and there weren't enough secret followers to save him. The voting proceeded from youngest to eldest, according to law, except that Caiaphas and others had already stated their positions, again a deviation from the law. This law prevented the older and more experienced members from influencing the voting of the younger Council members. So the voices echoed one another, "Guilty," "Guilty," "Guilty," with only a few antiphonal "not guilties" to break the pattern. Just as Judas feared, the decision was not close enough to effect an acquittal.

When the last person had voted, Caiaphas said, "The vote has been taken. Jesus, son of Joseph of Nazareth, has been found guilty of blasphemy, punishable by death. Now we must take him to Pilate. By our law he is condemned, but that is not enough, as you well know. Only Pilate can pass sentence of death. We must do our best to convince him that we have judged rightly."

"And how will we do this? What will be our argument?" someone spoke out.

"Whether or not Jesus is the Christ makes no difference to Rome," spoke another.

Annas, who had been observing the proceedings, suggested, "We can tell him that Jesus has stirred up the people, causing dissension in our nation. He forbids us to pay our taxes to Caesar, and he claims to be the Christ, the king."

"Well said," commended a member of the Council. "I am in favor."

And so they agreed together, and together they brought Jesus before Pilate.

Judas left the palace to go… where? He didn't know. He just started walking and thinking. He felt wretched, sick at heart. He had betrayed his Master and friend into the hands of these unscrupulous leaders, the very people that the Jewish nation looked to as their models. He thought he had done the right thing. How could he have been so wrong? The thirty pieces of silver weighed heavily in the pouch hanging from his girdle. The heaviness of his heart equaled that of his pouch, and the heavier one became so also became the other. It got more unbearable with every step he took. As he walked aimlessly, weighed down by his guilt and grief, and by the silver symbols of his treachery, he suddenly knew what he would do. He turned and hastened his steps. When he entered the temple, he approached the chief priests and the elders and said, "I have sinned in betraying innocent blood."

"What is that to us?" they replied coldly. "It is your sin. We have nothing to do with it or with you." So spoke those who were the guardians of the souls of Israel.

He regarded them with shock. They had conspired together. Would they reject him now? As he stood there the chief priests and elders turned away, dismissing him. Angrily he threw the money down at their feet and left.

An elder picked up the pouch and handed it to one of the chief priests. Thoughtfully he turned the coins onto the table, counting them. They were all there—thirty pieces of silver, money from the treasury, money that was now desecrated.

"This money cannot lawfully be put back into the treasury since it is blood money."

Another of the priests agreed and then suggested, "Let's buy a field for the burying of strangers."

So it was agreed; so it was done.

When Judas left the temple, he was distraught. He hated himself. The return of the money had not alleviated his guilt. If anything, it had become more intolerable. He could not live any longer with the knowledge of his sin, the betrayal of the best friend he ever had. The enormity of his deed exceeded his power to cope. Despite his remorse, he could not find forgiveness. The hopelessness of his situation drove him as he hurried with ever-quickening steps through the Lower City, out the Water Gate, and down into the Kidron Valley. Without giving himself any more time for reflection and self-condemnation, he found a strong vine, which he used to hang himself from a tree.

Chapter Eleven

Trial

It was very early on Friday morning. The happy group who had celebrated Passover in Elian's workroom was eating a bit of breakfast. During a lull in the camaraderie, Mary heard the distant sound of running feet. Closer and closer they came, pounding ever louder, keeping time with the loud beating of her heart. For no rational reason she feared it was bad news, and that the news was meant for her. *Not necessarily*, she quickly admonished herself. *Why should I make such an assumption? Runners bring good news too.* But her reasoning brought her no comfort. The overwhelming uneasiness she had experienced these past several days would not allow her to think of anything but trouble. She was too worried about Jesus to be influenced by positive thoughts. As a wanted man he was totally vulnerable, and anything could have happened.

Without stopping to knock first, John burst into Elian's shop, breathless, perspiring, and flushed. He dropped to the floor and sat cross-legged as he accepted the cup of water that Maria held out to him. When he had regained enough breath to talk, he looked at Mary and spoke hoarsely, "You must come with me—now! We must go immediately; there is no time to lose. It may already be too late."

"What are you talking about, John? Too late for what?"

"I'll tell you as we go. I don't know all the answers myself. All I know is that Jesus is in serious trouble, and we need to be there to help him."

"Oh, no! Oh, John, I knew it; I felt it this very morning." Mary sounded as though she would cry, but she could not.

"You go on with John, Mary," Maria told her. "You must go immediately."

"Yes," Martha agreed. "You go now. We will follow soon and find you. Hurry."

Mary looked at John and saw her own sad feelings reflected in his eyes. How he loved Jesus! Then she humbly did as she was told. She changed quickly into street clothes and hurried out with John, leaving behind her concerned and sympathetic friends.

Having reached the road that would take them to the Upper City and Caiaphas' palace, Mary could wait no longer. "Where are we going?"

"To the house of Caiaphas. Peter and I went there, hoping we could learn something."

"And that's where Jesus is?"

"Yes," John answered. "They took him there last night."

"Who?"

"The guards from Caiaphas' house came to Gethsemane where we had all gone with Jesus. They arrested him and took him to Caiaphas. Peter waited in the courtyard while I went inside. It was terrible. They condemned him. In the middle of the night, without agreement between witnesses, without even a real trial, they condemned him to death. They planned to call the Sanhedrin together at dawn to formalize their premature sentence. When they reached their decision, I went out to tell

Peter what had happened, and he was gone. No one knew his whereabouts, but someone said he went mad with grief and ran off. I have no idea where he might be. I've been looking for him ever since. Then I decided you should probably know what happened. I don't know that we can do anything though, except be there."

"That's all right. You were right in coming for me. Now, please, John, tell me what happened last night that Jesus was so vulnerable to arrest." Mary pleaded with him, hoping to make sense out of the senseless.

"Well, I'll have to start at the beginning," John replied. "The whole night was full of unexpected events. As you know, we planned to eat the Passover together in Jerusalem at the house of Josiah, the linen merchant. But we didn't celebrate the usual ritual. Jesus led us in a different way."

"How could it be different? It is prescribed, what we must do." Mary was perplexed, unable to imagine how it could be different, though she was not at all surprised that Jesus had made it so. He had been reinterpreting their laws for a long time, which explained why he was in such a predicament now.

"We started out as usual," he replied. "When it came time to bless the bread, Jesus took a piece and said the blessing. But when he broke it into pieces and gave it to us to eat, he called it his body." John said this with wonder, then added, almost in an undertone, "Strange, very strange."

"Go on," Mary prodded. "Then what?"

"Well. . ." John brought himself back to the present moment. "Then he picked up his chalice and offered the prayer of thanksgiving. After taking a sip, he passed it around to all of us to drink. When we had done that, he told us that this was his blood of the covenant, poured out for many. He said he would not drink wine again until he drank it in the kingdom of God."

There it was again—the kingdom of God. Mary wished she could grasp its full meaning, the meaning that Jesus intended. And what could he have meant—my body broken—blood poured out for many?

John continued, "Then he told us that one of us was going to betray him. We couldn't believe our ears. Each one kept asking him, 'Is it I?' 'Is it I?' He had in his hand a bit of unleavened bread. As he dipped it into the charosheth, he told us his betrayer was the person with whom he dipped the sop. It was Judas!"

"Judas!" interrupted Mary. "Yes," after a pause, "as I think back on it, he acted rather odd the other night in Bethany. I remember he seemed not to want to look at me. But to turn on Jesus? Would he really do such a thing?"

John shrugged his shoulders. "We don't know. In fact, in spite of Jesus and Judas dipping the sop together, it didn't register. I guess it seemed so impossible that any one of us would even think of turning on our Master. Even when Judas left, we still didn't understand. It never occurred to any of us that he went out to have Jesus arrested. I thought he went to the temple to give our Passover offering. Not until he came to the garden did the truth hit me.

"After Judas left, I'm ashamed to admit that we got into an argument about which of us was the most important. Jesus took an ewer of water and washed and dried our feet. We all felt uncomfortable about it, and Peter even tried to resist, but Jesus insisted. He told us we would not understand now what he was doing, but later we would, and that we must learn to serve one another. Needless to say, the argument ended. I don't think it will ever be an issue among us again. It was rather humbling, and thought provoking, to have our Master bathe our feet."

The two walked on in silence, brooding on John's words. Shortly he resumed. "Then Jesus told us many things about what we should expect in the future as his disciples. He told us we would all fall away from him and that Peter would actually deny him, which Peter soundly rejected. You know Peter—loyal as they come and absolutely certain that nothing could ever change that. But Jesus was unyielding. He insisted it would be so in spite of all of our protestations. The sad thing is that it has already happened."

"What do you mean?"

"Since last night in the garden I have seen no one. We all ran away. Only Peter and I followed, but we were very careful not to be detected. And now I can't even find Peter. And what about me? I didn't stay with him. I didn't try to defend him last night at that farcical trial. I stayed in the shadows to watch, just as guilty as Judas who was also there, keeping out of sight. He didn't want to be seen, it seemed to me, even though he was one of them."

"You mustn't be so hard on yourself. What happened was frightening."

"But he was right. And none of us wanted him to be right."

"You are here now, John, and we will find him. At least he will know he is not alone. Go on with your story."

"Someone started singing a psalm, and we all joined in, then we went out to the Mount of Olives. You know how he likes to pray in Gethsemane. When we got there he took three of us with him to a more secluded area. His manner became very troubled, even agitated, and he told us to wait there for him and to watch. To watch for what I didn't know, but obviously he expected something to happen and wanted to be warned. He went even farther off by himself to pray. Sad to say, we didn't do much watching. We were so tired, we immediately fell asleep. Three times he came back to us and found us sleeping. He was not angry, but I know he was disappointed in us.

"The third time, while he talked to us, Judas brought some temple guards into the grove, as I already mentioned. When they said they were looking for Jesus, he turned himself over to them—no argument, no struggle, just submission. When Peter realized what was happening, he became excited and angry and cut off the ear of one of the slave boys, which Jesus healed immediately. The men then bound him and led him away. Right after that we all decided we had better get out of there."

As he recounted the events of the previous night, John's voice broke. He choked back the tears and continued.

"Peter and I followed to see where they would take him. When I went into Caiaphas' house, I was appalled to see that Caiaphas had called together only a select group, those who have been strongly opposed to Jesus. And before my eyes they put him on trial, though I suppose technically it wasn't considered a trial since they are convening again, probably right now. But it may as well have been since they conducted it as such."

"But this was against our law," Mary protested. "A man cannot be tried at night. Besides, where were the witnesses for his defense?"

Mary couldn't understand the absence of normal procedure. These men, who made such an issue of obedience to every minute detail of the law, had made a mockery of the law, easily disregarding what didn't fit into their schemes.

"Yes, you're right about that, but it's what happened. There were no witnesses for his defense. The Sanhedrin acted as prosecutor, judge, and jury—very irregular indeed. I waited all night, hoping someone with some authority would call a halt to such blatantly illegal proceedings. But it never happened, and it looked as though things would not improve by morning. I can only hope that in this morning's proceedings some of those who have found themselves sympathetic will see to a fair and legal trial."

They came at last to Caiaphas' house, but no one was there. John asked the girl at the gate where everyone had gone.

"To the praetorium. I heard someone talking about it as they passed by."

This was bad news because that meant the trial had moved quickly to its conclusion, and the fact that they had gone to Pilate could only mean they sought the death sentence.

So the two hurried there as quickly as possible. When they arrived, they found Pilate holding court in the courtyard since the Jews were not allowed to enter a Gentile building.

Standing above them on a balcony, Pilate asked, "What accusation do you bring against this man?"

John recognized this as the opening sentence in a Roman trial. Obviously they had missed nothing here.

"Insurrection," Jotham stated. "We have already tried him in our Council and found him guilty in regard to our own laws. We believe he is guilty by Roman law also. We desire the death sentence but, as you know, we are not permitted to execute anyone."

"What is your proof?"

Jotham answered, "He stirs up the people, making them rebellious. He has forbidden us to pay taxes to Caesar. And worst of all, he claims to be the Christ, the King."

Pilate turned aside to Jesus, who stood on the balcony, but behind Pilate. He spoke to him privately. "Are you the King of the Jews?"

"My kingdom is not of the world. If it were, no man would have power over me."

Pilate persisted. "So you are a king."

"You are the one who says it."

When Pilate turned to the people, he suggested they let Jesus go. The crowd, which had at first been little more than the Sanhedrin itself, had now increased by at least a hundred as the curious gathered to watch this public spectacle. Their reaction was a decided *no.*

"He has some strange ideas, but he is not a threat to Rome," Pilate stated.

"No, he is dangerous. We cannot let him go." An angry voice argued with Pilate.

"Why do you consider him dangerous? He speaks of a kingdom, but not of this world. What other world is there? He speaks only out of his own imagination." Pilate was disdainful. He himself did not believe in such myths. Even his own gods meant nothing to him. "He is harmless. I cannot find him guilty of any crime."

Pilate's conclusion angered Jotham. Pilate hadn't taken this problem seriously. He was toying with them. Again he said, "He stirs up the people. He teaches his heresies all through Judea, from Galilee even to Jerusalem. He must be stopped, or the people will become rebellious."

"Is Jesus a Galilean then?" Pilate asked.

"Yes, sir, he is."

"That means he is under Herod's jurisdiction. Herod is in Jerusalem now. I will send him there. He will oversee the case." Speaking to the guard, he instructed him to take Jesus to Herod.

Herod ordinarily spent most of his time in Tiberius but had come to Jerusalem because of the Feast. He had been forewarned some time earlier of Jesus and his dangerous words by some highly antagonistic Pharisees. As a result he had sent spies to mingle with the crowds and report on Jesus' activities. At one point he became so concerned with Jesus' possible rivalry for his throne that he called his council together to determine a course of action.

It was hard to know just how Herod would handle the situation when Jesus was brought before him. Even though he had been told he had reason to fear him as a pretender to his throne, Herod also had a great curiosity about Jesus. The reports of his spies intrigued him. The man apparently did miracles, and Herod always wanted to be entertained. A remarkable occurrence would amuse him. The proceedings and the outcome would depend entirely on his mood at the moment.

When Jesus stood before Herod, he did so in silence, in spite of the many questions Herod asked.

"Are you a magician? A king? What is your title? How do you do the miracles you do? Show me a miracle, O king. It would please me immensely. Are you listening? I want to see something impossible." He spoke this last request with a growing anger. Herod was not used to being ignored.

The chief priests standing by were dismayed. This supposed trial quickly became a travesty. Herod was not taking the matter any more seriously than Pilate had; if anything, less so. And so they tried to bring things back to their own perspective by restating the charges. "He stirs up the people. All of Galilee has gone after him. He claims to be our Messiah. He wants your throne. Only you can put an end to all of this."

But Herod ignored them. Today he wanted to be entertained; he didn't want to be bothered with politics. He wanted a miracle.

Jesus continued to stand wordless. Herod's anger erupted. "So you call yourself a king. We will make you a king." He allowed the soldiers to array Jesus in splendid royal finery. Then he joined them in their sport as they mocked him and treated him with contempt. When he had tired of this sport, and his anger was spent, he sent him back to Pilate.

As they returned to the praetorium, Mary leaned heavily on John's arm. They had followed the crowd to Herod's palace. All this chasing around, and the uncertainty, and the pain of watching their beloved Jesus so shamefully treated exacted a huge emotional toll on them both.

John worried about Mary. She suddenly seemed very frail. *She shouldn't be here. I never should have brought her. Why didn't I think first?* he thought, then asked, "Do you want me to take you home so you can stay with my mother? You are exhausted.

Then I'll stay with him, and as soon as I can, I'll come back to you."

"*No*!" Mary's response exploded from her. More calmly she said, "I'm sorry, but I have to stay. I have to see what happens to my son. He is remaining strong. I can do no less."

"Yes. Yes, I understand. Come then, and lean on me." John knew he couldn't argue with her.

As they came to the praetorium, they found the crowd had doubled in size as more and more curious people had joined them. The large number of people moving from the praetorium to Herod's palace and back again could not fail to attract others. Now the courtyard overflowed into the street. They heard the murmuring and felt a strong undercurrent of violence about to erupt. The dark and sinister mood of the crowd frightened them. Mary wanted to be anywhere else but here, but she would not think of leaving.

When Pilate had taken his place on the balcony, with Jesus standing behind him, he spoke to the priests and the people.

"You brought me this man as one who perverted the people. After examining him, I did not find him guilty of any of your charges, and neither did Herod since he has sent him back to me. He has done nothing deserving of death. Therefore I will chastise him and release him."

"No!" they all cried as one voice.

"Take him away. If you must release someone, as you usually do during Passover, let it be Barabbas. Give us Barabbas instead," Jotham shouted.

"Yes. Barabbas. Barabbas." The shouts came from many voices in the crowd.

"But he is a dangerous man. He has murdered." Pilate found their demand incredulous. These people had gone mad. "You want such a man free instead of this one who is harmless?"

"Release Barabbas! Release Barabbas! Release Barabbas!" It became a chant.

"Then what shall I do with Jesus?"

"Crucify him. Crucify him!" They were becoming hoarse from their angry shouting.

"Release Barabbas and crucify Jesus! That's what we want you to do with Jesus!" shouted the man standing next to Mary, and she recoiled.

She could not believe it. *It just can't be that so many people hate Jesus enough to want him dead. Jesus healed them and fed them and loved them. Why would they want to put an end to all of this?* As she became aware of faces about her, Mary realized that she did not recognize a single one. *Where are his friends? Where are the people he befriended and who loved him? Where are the friends I just left, who said they would find me? These faces are filled with hate. These are not the same people who always follow him around like little children. They couldn't be. But then, if they are, what changed them?*

Then she heard it—the sound of the lash as it whipped through the air, whistling in the wind it created. That sound ended as bits of jagged, broken bone and lead found their mark against Jesus' back. Mercifully she could not see, since he had been taken from the balcony to another area of the praetorium, but she knew how his flesh was being savagely torn. Often victims did not survive a Roman flogging. When once she had the misfortune to witness the event, she had heard the cries of pain such punishment had drawn out of a strong man. But Jesus did not cry out; she heard no sound other than the cruelly repetitious lash. Feeling faint, she leaned more heavily on John.

Pilate returned to the balcony and spoke to the hostile crowd, "I am bringing him before you again so that you will know I can find him guilty of no crime." And when the soldiers brought him to Pilate, he announced, "Here is the man."

The crowd had no pity but was moved to ever greater wrath. "Crucify him! Crucify! Crucify! Crucify! Crucify!"

Pilate was exasperated. He could not, as a representative of Roman justice, crucify a man in whom he could find no guilt.

But neither could he afford to rouse the rage of the Jews against himself. So he did the expedient thing. He conceded.

"All right then, you take him and crucify him yourselves. I cannot convict him of any crime."

But the angry, relentless mob would not accept this. In fact, they could not since the Jews did not have the power of death over any man in this Roman-dominated country. Jotham shouted at Pilate, "We have a law by which this man must die. He has called himself the Son of God. This is blasphemy and punishable by death. But you know we cannot execute anyone by our own power and authority."

At last Pilate saw the truth of it all. These men were using him. But he was more frightened than anything else, too frightened even to be angry. Superstitious beliefs plagued him. He was not a religious man. He had no time for such foolishness. He could not believe that any being had all knowledge and all power over human beings, especially an invisible being. Might was power. The Romans had proved that as, by their might, they had conquered and now controlled almost the whole known world. Neither invisible gods nor idols of any shape had might. Yet one could never be completely certain that there was no supernatural being in control.

Pilate was wary, however. His superstitions kept him from being totally unbelieving, though he would never admit it. Signs that just might have come from the supernatural, just in case they were possible, kept him from true and total atheism. He worried now. Just this morning his wife had told him of a dream she had had. She had interpreted it to mean that only trouble could come from his involvement in this unusual trial. She had given him momentary pause before he had waved it off as meaningless. But now—now the truth was out. These people really wanted Jesus crucified because he claimed to be the Son of God—and it scared them. It scared even those who did believe in a supernatural God.

This stirred up Pilate's superstitions. Maybe he should have listened to Claudia. Perhaps his involvement would bring personal disaster. It was possible, though only barely, he reassured himself, that this God might have some power over him. He determined to find an end to this dilemma, so he questioned Jesus more closely.

"Where are you from?"

Receiving no response, he became impatient. "You refuse to speak to me? Don't you know that I have the power of life and death over you?"

Jesus then responded, "You have no power at all over me except that which has been given to you from above. The ones who have brought me to you have committed the greater sin."

Jesus' answer did not settle anything in Pilate's mind. He had all the power of Rome behind him, and this man—condemned by his own people—told him he had no power except what this invisible God had given him. He didn't think he could risk himself for the sake of his avowed atheism. He could not allow this man to die. He was a mystery, and his very mystery made Pilate unsure of exactly what he did believe. So Pilate again besought the crowd to allow him to release the guiltless Jesus, but they would not hear of it.

"He has made himself king over us. If you release him, you are no friend of Caesar's, for anyone who claims to be king is a threat to Caesar, whom you are sworn to protect." Getting desperate, Asa appealed to Pilate's fear of Caesar.

At these words Pilate brought Jesus to the edge of the balcony to show him to the people. The crowd went berserk, resuming its hateful cry.

"Crucify... crucify... crucify... crucify!"

"Shall I crucify your king?" Pilate made one last appeal to their good sense. But they had none. They believed only that Jesus was a threat to them politically. The Jewish authorities chose to believe this, though in reality they knew only their narrow religious hierarchy was threatened. The crowd believed this, at the moment, because they were fickle and easily swayed by every new wind, every convincing voice.

"We have no king but Caesar."

Unable to resist this seemingly demented crowd, Pilate relented. Washing his hands in a basin brought by a slave, absolving himself of guilt in the manner of the Jews, he said, "I am innocent of this man's blood. It is your responsibility."

From the crowd came, "His blood be on us and our children."

Satisfied that the guilt of shedding an innocent man's blood would not burden him, he commanded the guards to release Barabbas and to crucify Jesus.

So the guards took Jesus inside while the crowd cheered its victory. In a short while they returned leading their doomed prisoner. One of the guards, in a loud, mocking voice, announced, "Behold! Your king!"

When Mary saw what they had done to her precious son, her heart was wrung by the pain of such a spectacle. She fell to her knees, sobbing convulsively. "How much can he bear? How much can I bear?" For the sight that met her eyes was that of her eldest son standing painfully, but meekly, silently, dressed in a robe of purple, hands bound, his head crowned with a wreath of thorns. The blood trickled slowly from the wounds about his brow.

"John, I must go, *now!* I cannot bear this longer." And so with great difficulty they pushed their way out through the throngs and back to the street. They started away, going nowhere in particular—just away.

When they had put enough distance between themselves and the insanity of Pilate's courtyard that the screeching, angry voices had subsided to only an indistinct rumble, they sat down by the roadside, exhausted, defeated, lost.

Chapter Twelve

Agony

The motley group trudged through the marketplace, wending its way through every narrow street. This complied with the Roman law requiring that a condemned criminal be exposed to as many people as possible as an example. Mary moved along with them, acutely aware of activity all about—the pushing and shoving of the crowd, the haggling of the shoppers, the hawking of the merchants.

The smells that assailed her began to nauseate her—meat hanging in the open air, olives, oranges, onions and garlic, cooking food, livestock and animal skins, and who knew what else blended together in a sickening odor. Sick at heart, she wilted in the stifling heat. Too many perspiring bodies crammed into too small a space on this uncommonly warm day. She longed for the relative quiet of Nazareth and the comforting presence of her family.

No! she admonished herself. *I will not even think of that. My child needs me to be here.* Even though she knew that she could do absolutely nothing, her presence was important. Even if he didn't know she was there, she knew it. If she left, she would never forgive herself for deserting him.

They kept moving ahead, ever so slowly. The centurion had difficulty making headway through the vast hordes that filled the streets. Interested bystanders wanted a good look at what was happening in their midst. Shopkeepers stopped their hawking in mid-sentence, and shoppers lay down goods they were inspecting as they all turned to stare at the approaching spectacle. They had seen the Romans march prisoners past their shops many times before. Usually the condemned one was defiant, struggling, or cursing under the weight of his own cross and the prospect of a painful end, as was one of the three prisoners today. Or sometimes he was a bundle of terrified nerves, as was another of them, who stumbled along with tears streaming down his face. But never had they seen one such as the third prisoner. He was meekly quiet, not belligerently struggling against his guards. He was pale-faced but calm; one could even say resolute.

This must be the man Jesus. Those who had heard him knew he was not treasonous; those who had only heard of him—well, what was one to believe when all sorts of stories were abroad? He must have done something wrong, or why was he here, being hauled off to his death? Some merchants and shoppers along the way saw the opportunity for entertainment and joined the group bound for Golgotha, adding their own taunts and insults. Others, those who had seen and heard and believed Jesus, fell speechless, unable to believe the sight before them. These too followed along, sorrowfully.

On and on they walked; it seemed that they would never reach the gate leading out of the city. Mary wanted so much to reach out to Jesus. If only she could help him in some way. If she could do something to ease his pain and sorrow, it would also ease her own sense of helplessness. How utterly exhausted he looked. He had been through so much. Someone had mercifully removed that horrible crown of thorns, but his hair was matted with blood. Now he wore a crown of thick black clots around his brow where each thorn had pierced his head. He was weary, oh so weary, from lack of sleep, from lack of food, from loss of blood, from the beating and the lashing. She did not see how he could possibly make it all the way to Golgotha. She wept for her son, as she had done periodically ever since John apprised her of the perilous situation Jesus faced.

Where are all the disciples? She couldn't help but wonder, since they were seldom far from him. John had told her how they had all run away, and they certainly hadn't seen any of them in their futile jaunts from trial to trial. Surely they knew what was happening now, surely they would be somewhere close by. She had looked about now and again, but she did not see any of them. *And where is John? I haven't seen him anywhere since he returned to the praetorium.* After they had left the crowd earlier, he had decided to go back so he could see what they did with Jesus. Then when she had heard the noise of the crowd as it came to the bazaar, she had followed that. She knew John wouldn't be able to find her easily, but she couldn't wait for him; she had to stay close to her son.

Someone touched Mary's arm. She looked into the face of Mary Magdalene, her clothing in disarray, her hair disheveled, her face streaked with a mixture of tears and road dust. Jesus had freed her of demon possession many months ago. Mary, from the town of Magdala, had found new life and from that time had been a faithful follower.

"Mary!" Tenderly her name was spoken. "Mary, you look so weary. Let me help you." Mary Magdalene placed a strong arm around her waist to help her along. Mary appreciated the presence of this younger woman, but she could smile only feebly. Words failed them at such a moment. Overwhelmed by emotions, they held each other and sobbed unabashedly together. Protecting each other from the world about them, they sheltered themselves from the noise and the jostling of the crowd. Together they mourned until they were spent. Then in silence they allowed themselves to be moved along with the crowd, each supporting the other.

At last they reached the gate out of the city and started up the hill. The centurion tried to hurry his prisoners along. Mary noticed that he was reaching the end of his patience. His three charges moved along much too slowly. He kept turning on his horse, shouting at the soldiers, "Move it, men. Keep them moving. We haven't got all day!" Mary saw that the more the soldiers pushed, the more Jesus drooped and stumbled. A man whose body had experienced such punishment in the past few hours had no strength to carry such a heavy load.

Shortly, exasperated, the centurion stopped the procession. He sat for a moment, scanning the crowd until his eyes rested on a large, muscular man. He then laid the flat of his sword on the man's shoulder, impressing him into Roman service. "Take the prisoner's cross for him. He's too weak, and I'll not have him dead on his feet!"

Mary watched the swift succession of emotions cross the man's face—surprise, immediately followed by the intense fear anyone would experience when accosted by the inexorable power of Rome. This was in turn softened by compassion as he looked at Jesus. This stranger had been drawn into the suffering of Jesus. What a breath of fresh air—to find someone who cared, someone who could be kind in the midst of so much hostility. This man was such a one, a sensitive man. Mary felt he would have been a good disciple.

At the centurion's command Simon, as the man was called, leaped over to Jesus with such alacrity that Mary sensed that he had been feeling as helpless as she. He looked relieved that he could actually do something to help. He bent down, carefully lifted the cross from Jesus, and shifted it to his own shoulder. A groan escaped his lips as he bore its heavy weight.

Jesus stumbled on, relieved. With difficulty he straightened his bent back, stiff from the heavy weight of his burden and his recently inflicted wounds. He turned slowly, as if for the first time aware of the crowd around him. A great many women wept. She could see the love and pity in Jesus' eyes, in spite of his own pain, and heard the gentleness of his voice.

"Daughters of Jerusalem, don't weep for me, but for yourselves and for your children. For the days are coming when Jerusalem will be totally destroyed. The torture will be so great, the people will beg for death. Barren women will be glad they have no children. If they can do this to me who is innocent, what will they do to you, the guilty?"

Though Mary could not comprehend the meaning of such a prediction, she certainly sensed the pathos. Jesus had loved Jerusalem and been hurt by the rejection of its people, yet he grieved for them, and this in spite of what was happening to him. This terrible thing he saw for the future had no reality for her; her world had already crashed down around her. She would have been horrified if she had known that in less than forty years the Romans, with Vespasian first and then Titus to lead them, would destroy Jerusalem piece by piece and slaughter Jews until blood ran freely in the streets.

At long last they reached Golgotha.

The soldiers lost no time getting down to business, moving about with a brisk efficiency that showed how adept they were at their job. The centurion shouted orders as the soldiers prepared the crosses. They laid them out near their respective sites, attaching signs relating the crimes of each man.

In the meantime some women, in an act of mercy, came by and offered each of the condemned some myrrh to dull the pain. Jesus refused it, but the other two drank eagerly.

By now the crosses were ready. Jesus was placed on one of them, his arms outstretched. He who had endured so much through these many hours even now made no resistance. Mary couldn't bear to watch as they pounded those huge iron spikes into his flesh. She turned away, covering her eyes, but with every blow of the mallet she involuntarily groaned. Jesus moaned. Mary's heart was breaking—slowly, painfully breaking. Finally, the loudly reverberating ringing stopped, and the ringing in her ears died away too.

Just as she dared to look back at the horror-filled scene, the soldiers raised the cross into position. She watched in dismay as they dropped the cross into its hole with a body-shattering thud. Jesus' whole body twisted grotesquely; his head drooped low on his chest; blood slowly dripped from the wounds in his wrists and his feet; his breath came in great convulsive gasps. The sign above Jesus' head read, JESUS OF NAZARETH, THE KING OF THE JEWS in Hebrew, Latin, and Greek. That was his crime! That was the official word. She closed her eyes, but the scene would not be blotted out. She stood as though rooted to the ground. She could only stare in disbelief at what they had done to her son. The tears streamed unheeded down her face.

But what was this? *What is he saying?* Mary listened to the incomprehensible.

"Father, forgive them; for they don't know what they are doing."

He had no hate, only forgiveness. It was hard for Mary to imagine such forgiveness. No one could forgive people who not only tortured them, though they were innocent, but even enjoyed it. Yet Jesus did.

The taunts and disparaging words had not diminished in the slightest. *How can people be so hateful?* Mary wondered. *How can they be so discompassionate, even now when it is obvious that they are going to have what they want—his death? Is no one moved even to pity or remorse?* Mary couldn't understand such unreasonable, insane hatred. They couldn't resist scoffing at him, over and over, even trying to prove to themselves that he wasn't so great after all. Surely he would come down from the cross rather than die.

It seemed to give them great satisfaction to believe that because God had not saved him, he must not, after all, be the Christ. All around her she heard the voices of hate and derision.

"The Son of God? Ha! Wouldn't God save his own son? He's nothing but a blasphemer, the worst of sinners."

"He calls himself the Messiah. What Messiah would allow such a thing?"

"Come down and then we will believe."

Even one of the thieves jeered, "Save yourself—and us—if you can."

But then, in variance with the jeers came a word of faith, soothing, refreshing. The other thief had somehow sensed Jesus was indeed the Son of God. "Jesus, remember me when you come in your kingly power."

Mary was startled to hear such an expression of faith as this man obviously had. She found it amazing that he believed that death was not the end, and that Jesus would not be defeated by it. She wondered if the man had heard Jesus at some time and his words had had their effect on him. He had, after all, called him by name.

Again Jesus responded in love for another. "Truly I say to you, today you will be with me in Paradise."

Mary looked at her friends who had also, at some time, come to this scene of unspeakable horror. They were just as unbelieving and tear wracked as she that such a terrible thing could have happened to their beloved Jesus. John had found her here. Salome, his mother, had not been able to stay away. Neither had Mary Magdalene, nor she herself, nor any of the other women who had followed Jesus and his disciples from place to place. All these women had served them to free them for their busy ministry.

Mary, the wife of Cleopas, another of the faithful women, had come. She had more home responsibilities than the others as the wife of one of the members of Pilate's household, but what she could do for Jesus and his followers, she did. The whole family, including their sons, James and Joseph, had been drawn to Jesus. They never missed an opportunity to be with him as he went about preaching, teaching, and healing. And, of course, Mary of Magdala stood nearby. Mary felt a deep kinship with all of them, the kinship of mutual love for the same person.

Mary gradually became aware of a noise. Many noises surrounded her—the heckling of Jesus' enemies, the weeping of his friends, the cries of pain from the crosses, even the sad sound of the moaning wind—so it rather surprised her that one sound drew her attention at that moment, above all others. Perhaps because this new sound, an out-of-place sound, broke sharply into her bemused thoughts. It was the sound of clicking dice, accompanied by the laughing and cursing of the soldiers.

They had already divided among themselves his tunic, his girdle, his sandals, and his turban. This was their rightful bonus. Only his robe remained. They handled it, feeling the soft texture of the material, marveling that it was seamless. Each of them wanted it for himself, and so they gambled for it.

How she would like to have that robe! She had made it for him long ago, soon after he first left Nazareth. She had put many hours of work into that robe, and it pleased her to do it. Wherever he might be, Jesus would always have a little part of herself with him. She knew that he had something to warm him on cold nights. When at last she presented it to Jesus, she knew that he was touched by her expression of love and glad to have the robe. *Would that I could have that robe, something to hold on to when the pain of his loss overwhelms me. But it is not to be*, she thought, impatiently wiping the tears that blinded her vision.

Mary's eyes came back to Jesus, meeting his eyes. He was choking, trying desperately to get his breath, but even so, his eyes held hers and each reflected in the other the mingled feelings of love, pain, sorrow, and helplessness that each was experiencing. He looked straight at her and said slowly, carefully, between gasping breaths, "Woman,...behold... your... son." Calling John by name, he said, "John,... behold... your... mother." *Oh, how he does love me—to be concerned about me in these awful moments.* He had given her into the care of one he knew would love her as his own mother. The unrelenting tears began anew.

She looked at John. He was the youngest of all the disciples and the one whom Jesus had loved dearly. It was easy to understand that this might be so. John was a sensitive, loving young man, eager to listen to all that Jesus had to say and to learn from him. He was also contemplative. He seemed always to be pondering the meaning of what Jesus discussed with them. Jesus had often marveled at the depth of his thinking, revealed by the questions he constantly asked, especially for one so young. Yes, Jesus had made a good choice.

John also wept as he folded her into his arms. How could anyone who loved Jesus not be moved to tears? It was too terrible—too final! One could feel only horror at the torture and torment, frustration at being so helpless, unable to do anything but stand on this hill of desolation, watching as their whole world fell apart. There was only one release for such deep feeling and that was tears—hard, energy-draining, convulsing tears that came and went with every new realization of what was happening. Together they stood, surrounded and infused by the love of the others who stood there with them, watching as the scene continued to unfold.

They had been on the hill for about three hours when darkness suddenly came upon them, an unnatural darkness considering that it was only three in the afternoon. Some feared this strange darkness in the middle of the day and hurriedly left. Others feared but for a different reason. They knew that according to their religious law, the sun should not set upon one who had been executed. In spite of the earliness of the hour, they thought the sun was setting. Mary and her friends made no move to leave. They were no longer afraid. The time for that had passed when their fears had become reality in the crucifixion. So they stayed and waited.

"My God, my God, why have you left me?"

Mary knew how great must be the loneliness behind that forlorn cry. This was the first time Jesus had vented his own feelings, and oh, how agonized he was. Mary knew that this was the final and the worst torment. Not only had he been persecuted by his enemies and deserted by his disciples when he needed them most, but now he felt that even God had forsaken him. Aloneness could not be more complete.

"I am thirsty."

Jesus' voice, weak and hoarse, rasped across Mary's consciousness. Again she felt helpless. If only she could do something! How many times had she soothed his face, dirty and flushed from the intensity of playing in the hot sun, with nothing more than the hem of her sleeve touched quickly to her tongue for moisture? Why not now to bring relief to his parched tongue? Unmindful that she had no hope of reaching him, she nevertheless started to go to him. Suddenly she felt a firm grip on her shoulder and turned to look into the face of a soldier. He pushed her roughly away, telling her to keep back. Instead, another soldier filled a sponge with vinegar and water, stuck it onto a reed, and laughingly put it to Jesus' lips. Mary's tears came again in great wracking sobs. John once again held her protectively, and she wept unrestrainedly against his shoulder.

From the cross came a sigh, and with supreme effort Jesus shouted, "Finished." Then faintly, for his strength had ebbed, "Father, into... thy hands... I commit... my... spirit."

The words came with great difficulty, his life's breath almost gone. He gave one final convulsive gasp, and Mary knew her son was dead.

A new feeling came over Mary. She couldn't identify it, perhaps because it wasn't a single feeling. Jesus was gone and she felt an emptiness that she hadn't known since Joseph's death.

She knew that something very precious had just gone out of her life, and her life would never be the same again. But she also felt relief. She knew that Jesus was no longer suffering. His death, which had come more quickly than was usual by crucifixion, was merciful in that respect, and for that reason she was grateful.

Suddenly the earth shook, rocks were split, lightning pierced the black sky with long, jagged spears of blue-white light. They clung together, the five of them, trying to comfort and protect one another. And when it ended as quickly as it had come, Mary heard the centurion say, "Truly, this man was a son of God! This man was innocent!" And he fell to the ground, beating his breast. "God forgive me! Please, God, forgive me!" Mary knew he would be forgiven. Hadn't Jesus already also asked it of God?

Because nightfall was almost upon them and the bodies of the three men had to be taken down and buried, some of the Jewish leaders requested that their legs be broken to hasten death. So the soldiers set about to do this one final task, but when they came to Jesus, they found that he was already dead. One of them stabbed him in the side instead. Blood and water gushed out of this new wound, reminding Mary of her purification ceremony in the temple in Jerusalem when Jesus was six weeks old. There, a very old man, whose name was Simeon, had seen them. His face had lit up as he took her tiny baby into his arms. She knew he had recognized Jesus as the Messiah. His words, which she remembered now, had seemed strange at that time.

"...and a sword will pierce through your own soul also..."

It was as he said.

She felt John's gentle touch on her elbow and knew that they must leave this place.

Chapter Thirteen

Reminiscence

Mary woke early on the Sabbath after a night of less sleep than wakefulness, with emptiness in her heart and a sick feeling in her stomach as she remembered the day before. Was it really only yesterday that Jesus had died? It felt as though an eternity had passed. She lay thinking of all that had transpired in such a few hours. Her beloved eldest son had been betrayed, condemned, convicted, and sentenced to death in less than twelve hours. His execution was immediate and cruel, though not in the least unique. Crosses along the highways, sometimes one alone, sometimes many together, were a common sight, grim reminders of the presence of an unyielding oppressor in their land. She felt tired, drained of energy. Somehow, it didn't seem real at all. It was as though she had been dreaming all those things that happened yesterday, though she knew full well they were real.

Before sundown the night before, Joseph, the Arimathean, whom she knew to be a secret disciple, came to tell her that he had taken Jesus' body and had prepared it for burial. With great relief she listened to what they had done because she had been unable to do what was necessary. Joseph himself had washed the bruised and broken body and anointed it with sweet-smelling oil. He told her how Nicodemus had helped him wrap Jesus in soft strips of linen and had sprinkled myrrh and aloes between the layers. Then they had placed Jesus in Joseph's own tomb, new and unused. Mary, grateful for his kindness, could not thank him enough.

Then, as she remembered all this, she decided to visit Joseph's garden. She didn't really know why she should go there except that she would be near her son's body, and that the garden was both beautiful and quiet—a good place to think. She desperately needed to be alone to sort out her jumbled thoughts. Once she had decided this, she dressed quickly and slipped quietly out of the house.

As she walked along the street, her mind wandered back almost thirty-four years to the early years of Jesus' life. She had been very young then, and many wonderful and strange things had come to pass. His birth had been announced by an angel who had told her that this child would be a king, the Son of God. When that birth had finally occurred, it was heralded by hosts of angels. Shepherds had come from the fields to see this wonderful child; even strange and wise men from faraway places had come to bring him gifts because they knew there was something special about him. Except for the fear of Herod that drove them to Egypt, those first years were exciting. After their return to Nazareth their lives had reverted back to their normal, uneventful patterns.

Throughout Jesus' growing-up years Mary had often pondered the events surrounding his birth. She understood what the angel had said about him. He was the long-awaited Messiah of Israel. A rather ordinary girl and not at all a queen, Mary would be the mother of the king. Jesus would save the nation from her enemies and make her great again. More than that, he was the Son of God.

Between the angel's visit and the birth of Jesus, she had frequently speculated as to the nature of such a child. Would he be a perfect child—never crying, never angry, never quarrelsome, never disobedient but always kind, obedient, helpful? She was glad that he was not really different from other children. He had grown up like any normal, active little boy.

Jesus had been such a strong, sturdy, bright little boy. Even from the time he could crawl, Jesus loved to be with Joseph in the workshop, which gave his father great pleasure. He used to sit among the shavings and the sawdust, building precarious pyramids from the little scraps that Joseph gave him. When they fell, he laughed and built them up again. As he got a little older, he sometimes became frustrated and cried when his creations would not stay together as did Joseph's. By the time he was three, he showed amazing dexterity and strength. He actually hammered the little wooden pegs into his scraps of wood after Joseph bored the necessary holes. He was always so proud of himself when he could make them go all the way into the wood without breaking them. He never lost interest in working with Joseph, in learning how to become an accomplished carpenter. By the time he was twelve years old, the two of them were working side by side.

That year he caused them the only real anxiety of his young life. They had gone to Jerusalem for his twelfth birthday to celebrate Passover. All went well until it was time to return to Nazareth. Unknown to them, he had not left Jerusalem with their caravan. A whole day passed before they realized he was not among their group of pilgrims. They lost five days as a result of having to return to the city to find him and were extremely anxious about his whereabouts. He had not seemed sorry for causing them anguish but rather had seemed very sure of the rightness of his actions, and even somewhat surprised that they did not understand. After they had overcome their initial angry reactions and were once again on their way, she and Joseph could only wonder between themselves the meaning of his words. "Why did you search for me? Didn't you know that I must be in my Father's house?"

He had grown up to be a responsible young man, well liked by everyone who knew him. His ability to take over Joseph's work after his death had been a tremendous relief to her. Even as young as he was, he had been able to help fill a father's role for the other children, and she had been grateful for this also. Yes, life had seemed to be no different than before the angel's visit for so long that she had even begun to wonder what the angel's announcement had really meant and how it could possibly be related to the prophets' foretelling of the Messiah.

By this time Mary had reached Joseph's garden, a beautiful and peaceful spot. The small olive grove beyond with its grayish-green leaves provided a soft backdrop for the dark brown of the bare grape vines that covered the whole area in neat rows. Two almond trees crowned with snowy white blossoms stood proud in their delicate beauty. What a contrast to the darkness of yesterday up on that desolate hill. Just a few feet from the almond trees, she noticed a grape press and walked to it. It was far enough from Jesus' grave that she would not be noticed by the guards, yet she could still see it. She wanted to be nearby as she tried to think things through. She sat down on a large rock and began sorting out all the thoughts that filled her mind.

This man whom she now mourned, who lay so close and yet was so inaccessible, was the Messiah. She knew that, because she trusted God's word. His messenger, Gabriel, had told her so. Old Anna and Simeon had seen Jesus the time they were in the temple shortly after his birth. Through the Spirit of God, both had known that Jesus was the Promised One. She could not doubt; she had too much confirmation. But how could his death possibly help him to save the nation?

She knew well the prophecies regarding the Messiah. Isaiah had written much about him, as had Zechariah and Micah. All Jews knew these passages of hope, though she was perhaps more acutely familiar with them. Ever since the angel's visit she spent much time trying to discern the meaning of the many passages the prophets had written concerning the Messiah, though they were not easy to understand. Most of what characterized Jesus' life as being different from that of other men seemed to be spoken of by the prophets. Her mind moved back over the years, to the visit of the angel who told her that she had been chosen to be the mother of the Messiah. She could still hear Gabriel's words:

> He will be great, and will be called the Son of the Most High; and the Lord God will give to him the throne of his father David, and he will reign over the house of Jacob for ever; and of his kingdom there will be no end.

Isaiah had said that there would be a child born who would sit on the throne of David and establish his kingdom and maintain it forever—the same thing Gabriel had said. She remembered Joseph telling her how the angel had come to visit him in a dream when he was planning to divorce her. The words he said were the same ones Isaiah had used long ago: "Behold, a virgin shall conceive and bear a son, and shall call his name Immanuel." He had told Joseph that this child would save the people from their sins. Micah had said that the king would come from Bethlehem, and Jesus had indeed been born in Bethlehem despite the fact that they lived in Nazareth. Had it not been for the census required by Caesar Augustus, Jesus would have been born in Nazareth, but the prophecy had been fulfilled, and this was to her another proof of his messiahship.

Jesus himself had read a passage from the prophet Isaiah in the synagogue on one of his visits to Nazareth. He told the people that he was the one about whom the prophet was speaking.

> The Spirit of the Lord is upon me, because he has anointed me to preach good news to the poor. He has sent me to proclaim release to the captives and recovering of sight to the blind, to set at liberty those who are oppressed, to proclaim theacceptable year of the Lord.

How often she thought about this event. It was such a high moment for her and for all those listening to him in their synagogue. Everyone knew him as one of their own, a neighbor, a carpenter, and a man with the same poor background as the rest of them. They had waited so long, as had all Israel, for the one who was to do all these things. Now here he was among them and known to them all. Oh, what a glorious day it was for the little, insignificant village of Nazareth. God at last was going to avenge his people, and the one who was going to do it belonged to them.

How sadly mistaken they all were, and how sad the day turned out to be for Nazareth, and for me, as Rebekah and Judith so recently reminded me. Because then, when he sat down to teach, he said words that they could not accept. He had reminded them of how it was in ancient times when Elijah had been sent to help a widow in Sidon, and Elisha had healed the leprosy of Naaman, the Syrian, both of them Gentiles and therefore sinners. Jesus' audience had not liked being reminded that these hated Gentiles had received God's gifts and not his Israelite children. Perhaps they believed that Jesus told them it was about to happen again, that the Gentiles would also benefit from the coming of the anointed one. In any case, they were so angered they would have thrown him over the hill outside Nazareth if he had not somehow escaped. Mary shuddered at the memory.

Another passage came to her mind. Isaiah had also said:

> Then the eyes of the blind shall be opened, and the ears of the deaf unstopped; then shall the lame man leap like a hart, and the tongue of the dumb sing for joy.

This had indeed happened. Jesus had become well known as a healer. Yet another passage came to her, again from Isaiah:

> There shall come forth a shoot from the stump of Jesse, (*was not Jesse, the father of King David, an ancestor of Jesus?*) and a branch shall grow out of his roots. And the Spirit of the Lord shall rest upon him, the spirit of wisdom and understanding, the spirit of counsel and might, the spirit of knowledge and the fear of the Lord.

Yes, if ever there was a man who knew and obeyed God, Jesus had been that man!

Even the joyful event of just one week ago, related to her in such high excitement by Maria, was recorded by the prophet Zechariah.

> Lo, your king comes to you; triumphant and victorious is he, humble and riding on an ass, on a colt the foal of an ass.

Now she knew the prophecies that she had not understood, or perhaps did not want to, foretold the events of the day just past. Those men from long ago seemed to have leapt forward in time, witnessed these things, and returned to their own day to write them with such accuracy. Both Zechariah and Isaiah had described some of the tortures that Jesus had just suffered. But the one passage that stood out most vividly in Mary's mind came from Isaiah. She had been drawn to this passage often without realizing why, and she had engraved it on her heart. She couldn't imagine that it had anything to do with her, and she had tried to shove the awful words out of her mind. For some unknown reason those words seemed important for her life. Now she knew, and she shuddered as she recalled the words:

> Who has believed what we have heard? And to whom has the arm of the Lord been revealed? For he grew up before him like a young plant, and like a root out of dry ground; he had no form or comeliness that we should look at him, and no beauty that we should desire him. He was despised and rejected by men, a man of sorrows, and acquainted with grief; and as one from whom men hide their faces he was despised, and we esteemed him not. Surely he has borne our griefs and carried our sorrows: yet we esteemed him stricken, smitten by God, and afflicted.
>
> But he was wounded for our transgressions, he was bruised for our iniquities; upon him was the chastisement that made us whole, and with his stripes we are healed. All we like sheep have gone astray; we have turned every one to his own way; and the Lord has laid on him the iniquity of us all. He was oppressed, and he was afflicted, yet he opened not his mouth; like a lamb that is led to the slaughter, and like a sheep that before its shearers is dumb, so he opened not his mouth. By oppression and judgment he was taken away; and as for his generation, who considered that he was cut off out of the land of the living, stricken for the transgression of my people? And they made his grave with the wicked and with a rich man in his death, although he had done no violence, and there was no deceit in his mouth.

She mentally cringed at the pictures each phrase painted in her mind's eye. Isaiah wrote those words long, long ago, yet they perfectly described what happened to Jesus yesterday. He was certainly wounded and bruised. The pictures were vivid, too easily recalled—the wounds from thorn and lash—lash? From the lash come stripes, long gashes deep in the victim's back. "With his stripes we are healed," it said. As she pondered this, she thought she had a flicker of an answer. According to Hebrew belief, there was no forgiveness of sin without sacrifice. For centuries the blood of perfect lambs was shed for the forgiveness of sin. Jesus somehow became that lamb of sacrifice, the most perfect of them all. His life blood had been shed so that the sins of the people would be forgiven, bringing healing.

Reflecting on these complicated ideas, Mary began to come to terms with Jesus' shortened life and his seemingly senseless death. She could not move beyond the comparison of Jesus and the sacrificial lamb. Her thoughts on this image insisted on developing into something comprehensible and meaningful out of all the vileness. *This was something God planned,* she dared to think. The ways of God were a mystery to her, but she had learned a long time ago not to question his ways. *When God acts, there is no question but that only the best possible good can be the outcome. If God was acting here, then something good has to come out of this.* Somehow, now, she felt reassured, at least that there was a deeper, holier purpose behind all that had happened, that evil men had not been permitted to commit such horrendous acts of cowardice and cruelty for no good reason.

Mary was beginning to feel at peace. She felt now that she might be able to face the days ahead, adjust to life without her eldest son with the help of God. It would be hard and it would be lonely; she would miss him very much, but it would not be an unbearable, hopeless loneliness. As sad as it was, his death did have a purpose—an important, far-reaching purpose. She could accept that. And she was looking forward to learning what that purpose might be.

A bright-colored bird caught her attention and brought her out of her reverie. It was a bee-eater, the beautiful bird that sported so many colors—red, yellow, black, blue, and brown. Its coloring made her glad. She thought again about the beauty of this day and of the garden in contrast to yesterday's darkness and the bleakness of the hill. She compared the lightness of her heart now to its heaviness the day before. She turned her eyes to the bright blue sky above, and the heavens beyond, and thanked God for having brought her out of her despair. Feeling like a new person, she returned to her new home.

Chapter Fourteen

Joy

Through the veil of sleep Mary heard voices. As she forced herself awake, she discerned women's voices, high-pitched and excited, occasionally punctuated by the deeper tones of a man. For a few moments she felt disoriented. *Who are these people? What are they doing in my house, talking so loudly at this time of night?* She pushed herself up on one elbow and tried to get her bearings. Then she remembered this was not her house but the rented home of John and his mother. *The man's voice must be John's,* she decided. Someone had felt that something was important enough to awaken John before the first light of day. Sensing something strange, Mary got up to see what all the commotion was about. She found John just closing the door to the street, and Salome standing by him, dressed for the day, flushed and breathless. It was much too early for her to be up, let alone out on the streets.

"What is the matter?" Mary asked. "You're out and about so early, Salome."

"Yes. Mary of Magdala, Joanna, and I went early this morning to the tomb. Mary had bought more spices. We wanted to prepare Jesus' body properly. Everything was done so hurriedly on the sixth day, to finish before dusk." This was important because sundown marked the beginning of Sabbath.

Salome paused a moment, then continued uncertainly. "He was gone."

"Gone?" Mary's voice rasped hoarsely in her throat. "Gone? How could he be gone?"

"I don't know. I just don't know. The stone was rolled away. The guards were nowhere in sight. Jesus wasn't in the tomb. Mary said she saw him and that he even spoke to her. We didn't see him but…" Her voice trailed off into silence.

"Never mind," John said. "Mary couldn't have talked to him. She was dreaming. Peter and I will find out what happened."

With these words John, whose young body had sagged under the weight of unmanageable burdens, straightened his back. The determination to do something about this new problem, instead of just being bandied about by out-of-control circumstances, restored to him a sense of purpose.

"Peter is coming," he stated, "and we will go there to see for ourselves. Maybe something will be there that the women missed, and we can find out the truth. There has to be a simple explanation."

"Peter? What does he know about this?" Mary asked.

"We have already been to his lodging place. When we told him we were coming here, he said he would come by shortly. He and John will go together to the tomb."

As Salome spoke, someone pounded on the door with great force and obvious impatience. John opened it to Peter, and the two hurried out.

"Wait," Mary called to them. "I want to go with you."

"No," Peter insisted. "Wait here. We'll come back and tell you what we find out."

Mary, disheartened, stood rooted to the floor, staring at the closed door. "What is the meaning of this? Jesus' body gone? If indeed that is the truth, then someone must have stolen it. Why would anyone want to steal his body? And why would Mary say she talked to him? How could she have anyway?" She said this more to the air than to Salome.

Mary was forlorn. All of her hard-earned sense of acceptance that she had achieved seemed to be crumbling. She stood there silently, questions filling her mind. The whole thing seemed nothing less than preposterous. After some minutes had passed, she sat down on one of the mats on the floor and prepared herself to wait for however long it might be necessary. Salome understood Mary's pain and sat silently with her.

They waited about an hour for the return of the two men. When they finally came back, they added nothing more to what the women had already said, only that they had both gone into the tomb.

"But what was so strange," Peter said, almost as though talking to himself, "was that the linen cloths were lying there just as though he had been slipped right out of them. They seemed to be undisturbed. And the napkin that covered his face was neatly folded and lying separately, away from the rest of the linen. How could that be? How could anyone have removed his body without disturbing the linen wrappings?"

It was indeed a mystery. Mary found herself puzzled by it, but strangely, no longer upset. She did, however, have a very strong desire to visit the tomb herself.

"I must go there," she told her friends. "I have to see with my own eyes that he really isn't there."

"One of us should go with you," John offered.

Mary was grateful that he had not tried to stop her, but she didn't want company just then either. "No, please. I need to go alone." Mary's eyes were pleading.

Salome agreed. "Let her go. She will be all right. She just needs to try to find her own answers, just as you did."

John couldn't very well argue with that and so, with some reluctance, he let her go. Mary walked with as much speed as she could muster. She wished she were as young as Mary of Magdala so she could run, but even walking fast made her breath short. Fortunately she had not far to go. She hurried by the cistern and past the grape press where she had sat just yesterday. *Yes, the stone is gone, and so are the guards.* She ran as she approached the opening to the tomb, her fatigue forgotten, so great was her anticipation.

She bent to look in and saw just what Peter had described. It was indeed strange to see Jesus' burial cloths lying there as though he were in them. Obviously, however, he was not there. She could not bring herself to go all the way in, but stood just outside on the edge of the rut carved out for the great stone and contemplated the sight before her. She stood in the opening of the sepulcher for a long time. Finally, she went and sat on a nearby rock, wondering what this newest event, another extraordinary event, could possibly mean.

Mary let her mind wander back through the events of the past few days, and beyond, through the years so recently past. Events and words blended together and then separated in kaleidoscopic fashion. Certain things stood out, bidding her special attention. One event kept trying to come into focus. It happened not so very long ago, and it was only by chance that she even had the opportunity to hear of it.

Jesus and the disciples had been in Capernaum and traveled south, on their way back to Jerusalem. They had stopped one night in Nazareth, a dangerous thing for them to do, considering that her neighbors still harbored resentment against Jesus. But they arrived after dark; they needed to stop for the night, and so they had come to her little house on the hillside. She remembered how she had inquired of John about where they had been and what they had experienced. He told her about a very interesting conversation that had occurred in Caesarea Philippi.

Jesus had asked them if any of them knew who he was, and Peter had said, "You are the Christ, the Son of the living God." Jesus had then instructed the disciples not to tell anyone. He had also said something about the Son of man having to suffer much, and being killed, and then on the third day being raised. John was quite sure that Jesus spoke of his own death. While he didn't like to hear Jesus talk like that, he could see that it was certainly a possibility since there were those who didn't understand him and hated him enough to want him dead. But the part about being raised was incomprehensible to him, as it was to her, so much so that she had forgotten all about it.

Now she wondered, *This is the third day since the crucifixion. Is that what happened—was Jesus raised? What does that really mean—to be raised? Could it be that Jesus is actually alive now? Even though he was most certainly dead when we left Golgotha on that awful day, could it really be possible that he does live again? But how? Was it like Lazarus? He had been dead, and Jesus brought him back to life again. No one knew how; it just happened. Jesus told him to come out of that tomb, and he came out, though dead for four days! He was definitely alive; he was a person with a body, not a ghost.*

Hadn't she just been a guest in his home and seen this for herself? Mary became more and more excited. Her heart pounded within her. To think that Jesus might actually be alive! What a daring thing even to think. If she spoke it aloud, people would think her a lunatic.

Could this be some part of God's greater purpose—to have allowed Jesus to die but to live again? It could be. God's ways are not our ways. If it is so, there must be a reason. In spite of the questions, and the fear of the ridicule she would experience if she shared the possibility, her anticipation and joy would not be abated. Mary had no idea if she could contain it. But contain it she must, at least until she knew for sure that it was so.

With a spring in her stride Mary returned to John's house.

That same evening she went with John and Salome to the house of Jude. Word had spread among the other nine disciples, and they had agreed to meet at sundown. Only Thomas for some reason did not come. Other disciples beyond those of the Twelve, who were deeply concerned about the whereabouts of Jesus' body, also arrived there.

Everyone stood around uncertainly, conversing uneasily in whispers behind locked doors. Fearful of being discovered, they knew that the Pharisees or the Romans would accuse them of stealing the body. If found together in that room, they would be questioned, perhaps even tortured, as this was part of Roman justice. They faced a desperate situation. To make matters worse Mary Magdalene insisted that she had indeed seen Jesus and spoken with him. Salome and Johanna, though they had not seen him themselves, had come to believe Mary. They also tried to convince the others that she was telling the truth, that she had not been dreaming.

Mary was indecisive. Should she share the thoughts she had had that morning? Or should she remain silent? She had not seen Jesus, but she had felt in her heart that he was alive, and she believed these women. She did not believe that Mary of Magdala had imagined what she wanted to see, as many kept inferring. Finally Mary's belief in the impossible overcame her fear of ridicule, and she felt bolder as the women remained faithful to their story and would not allow themselves to be dismissed as foolish dreamers.

She spoke, "I know it is true. I have not seen him as Mary Magdalene has, but I…"

A cautious rap on the door interrupted Mary. Everyone in the room became instantly quiet, alert. Who could it be? Should they open the door? Peter quietly stepped to the door, listening.

"Open the door!" someone said in a loud whisper. "It's Cleopas and Mary."

A sigh of relief breathed through the room.

"Let us in, quickly. We have news!" the visitor insisted.

Peter hurriedly unlocked the door and let in the two.

"We have seen him! We have seen Jesus!" Cleopas could barely contain his excitement.

"How could you have seen him? Tell us," demanded Nathanael.

"We were on our way home to Emmaus this afternoon," Cleopas told them. "We discussed between ourselves the things that have happened this past week and especially the mystery of the empty tomb. As we were so engrossed in our conversation, we did not notice that a stranger had joined us until he asked what we were talking about. So we told him about all the things that had happened. I was somewhat amazed that he didn't know about all this himself. I decided he must be a traveler, newly arrived.

"He listened as we told the story then said to us, 'Wasn't it necessary for the Christ to suffer all these things and to enter into his glory?' We hadn't been talking about the Messiah, but he asked us that question. Then he told us about the Scriptures and prophecies that talk about the Messiah, beginning with Moses."

"We were impressed with how he knew the Scriptures so well," Mary interrupted. "Besides, the more he talked, the more we could see how all the things that happened to Jesus were the same things that the prophets had told us would happen to the Messiah."

"It was getting on toward evening by the time we arrived in Emmaus," Cleopas continued, "so we invited him to come in and eat supper with us, which he did. When we were at the table he took the bread, blessed it, and broke it, and immediately we recognized him. It was Jesus! He is alive!"

The group immediately abandoned all caution as the room fairly burst with the mingled sounds of awed delight and skeptical disbelief. Everyone started talking at once, and no one was listening to anyone.

John called for silence. When he had their attention, he reminded them all of something Jesus had once said. "Remember how at Caesarea-Philippi we knew for certain that Jesus is the Messiah? He told us not to tell anyone. But then he told us that the Son of man would suffer and die, and on the third day he would be raised. We didn't want to hear about his dying; it was too painful. What he said about being raised was meaningless to us then. So we have never thought in terms of his coming back to us, only that he would be taken away from us in the finality of death. But now Jesus has suffered and died, just as he said. This is the third day, and he is gone from his tomb. Why can't we believe that he has been raised up from death, also as he said?"

"Even so," agreed Cleopas, "and so you must believe us. We speak the truth. We are surely slow to believe what we don't understand. But you must believe. He spoke with us; then just as soon as we recognized him, he was gone from us—vanished into thin air, like a spirit."

Cleopas had hardly finished speaking when Jesus stood among them. This sudden appearance of a spirit frightened them all, leaving them speechless and trembling.

"Peace be with you, my beloved children. Why are you so disturbed within yourselves, and why do you question so much?" Jesus asked. "Do you not recognize me? Here. Look. Here are the nail prints in my wrists. Look at the scars in my feet. Are these not the marks of one who has been crucified?"

So overcome by the wonder of it, Jesus' friends could hardly believe what they saw. It couldn't be Jesus, really alive again. It had to be his spirit. Only spirits could move through closed doors.

So Jesus asked for something to eat, saying to them, "A spirit has not flesh and bones as you see that I have." Mary handed him a piece of broiled fish, which he ate for their benefit. He finally convinced them that he was actually alive, not just a spirit.

Elation filled the room. The fear of being discovered had vanished. The gloom of uncertainty had dissipated. The tears of bereavement had been wiped away. Unbounded joy had taken their place.

Quietly, in the midst of celebration, Jesus began to teach them as he had done so many times before, only this time they heard with real comprehension. "It has been written in the Scriptures that the Christ, the Messiah, should endure much suffering, be put to death, and come to life on the third day. It is also written that repentance and forgiveness of sins must be preached in the name of the Christ to all nations, beginning right here in Jerusalem. As the Father has sent me to do his will, even so I send you to do these things. Go and preach and teach and heal in my name even as I did these same things in the name of my Father who sent me."

Mary's heart overflowed. Her joy knew no bounds. Her faith in God's promises was strengthened. God had given her a difficult assignment when he chose her to be the mother of the Messiah. But he had not left her comfortless. He had never abandoned her to carry the burden alone. He had always been right there with her, making his strength her strength. Even in the darkest of days, he had given her the courage and the ability to endure, yet not just to endure, but to grow in her own faith. And now, wonder of wonders, he had restored her soul. He had brought joy out of her mourning. He had replaced the bitterness of her sorrow with the soothing oil of joy.

Reference Table

Chapter 1: Anticipation

Healing—Matt. 9:35, 12:15, 15:30; Mark 1:32–34; Luke 4:40; et al.

Forgiveness of sins—Matt. 9:2; Luke 5:20; et al.

Raising of Lazarus—John 11:30–44.

The Pharisees fear Jesus and want to stop his work—Mark 3:6, 11:18; Luke 6:11.

Prophet not honored in his own country—Matt. 13:57; Luke 4:24.

Gabriel announces Jesus' birth to Mary—Luke 1:30–33.

Jesus' brothers and sisters—Matt. 13:55; Mark 6:3.

Jesus' brothers unsympathetic—John 7:5.

Chapter 2: Coronation

Jesus sent out his disciples to do his work—Matt. 10; Mark 6:7–13; Luke 9:1–6.

Jesus tells two disciples to fetch donkeys—Matt. 21:1–2; Mark 11:1–3; Luke 19:30–31.

Triumphal entry—Matt. 21:8ff; Mark 11:7–10; Luke 19:36–38.
The stones would cry out—Luke 19:40.
"The whole world has gone after him"—John 12:19.
Jesus weeps over Jerusalem—Luke 19:41–44.
Love your enemies—Matt. 5:43–46; Luke 6:27–28.
Turn the other cheek—Matt. 5:39; Luke 6:29.
"Who is this man?"—Matt. 21:10.
Prophet Jesus—Matt. 21:11.
Jesus and the moneychangers—Matt. 21:12; Mark 11:15–17; Luke 19:45–46.
Healing after confrontation in the temple—Matt. 12:13.
Jesus stays in Bethany—Mark 11:11.

Chapter 3: Entrapment
Chief priests and scribes confer—Matt. 22:15.
Question of authority—Matt. 21:23–27; Mark 11:28–33; Luke 20:2–8.
Parable of vineyard and wicked servants—Matt. 21:33–43; Mark 12:1–11; Luke 20:9–18.
Isaiah's prophecy of vineyard destroyed—Isa. 5:5–6.
Moses' reminder to keep the commandments—Deut. 10:12–13.
Friends among the hierarchy—Mark 12:32–34; John 7:50, 19:39.
Including Joseph of Arimathea—Matt. 27:57; Mark 15:43; John 19:38.
"I will be your God" (Abraham)—Gen. 17:7.
"I will be your God" (Moses)—Exod. 6:7.
When they tried to arrest him, they feared the multitude—Matt. 21:46; Mark 12:12; Luke 20:19.
Paying taxes to Caesar—Matt. 22:17–22; Mark 12:14–17; Luke 20:22–25.

Whose wife, of seven brothers, is she?—Matt. 22:23–33; Mark 12:18–27; Luke 20:27–40.
Great commandment—Matt. 22:36–40; Mark 12:28–31.
Scribe's response and Jesus' comment—Mark 12:32–34.
"What do you think of the Christ?"—Matt. 22:42–45; Mark 12:35–37; Luke 20:41–44.
Beware of the scribes and Pharisees—Matt. 23:1–12; Mark 12:38–40; Luke 20:45–47.
Widow's mite—Mark 12:41–44; Luke 21:1–4.
Prophecy of destruction of temple—Matt. 24:1–2; Mark 13:1–2; Luke 21:5–6.
Caiaphas says, "It is expedient"—John 11:50, 18:14.

Chapter 4: Parables
Parable of the two sons—Matt. 21:28–32.
Parable of the marriage feast, wedding clothes—Matt. 22:1–14.
Parable of the talents—Matt. 25:14–30; Luke 19:12–27.
Parable of the sheep and the goats—Matt. 25:31–46.
Jesus predicts his own death, possibly on Bethany road—Matt. 26:2.
Hierarchy plots—"not during the feast"—Matt. 26:5; Mark 14:1–2.

Chapter 5: Bethany
Jesus anointed—Matt. 26:6–7; Mark 14:3.
By Mary of Bethany (Maria in this book)—John 12:1–8.
Judas leaves to betray Jesus—Matt. 26:14–16; Mark 14:10–11.
Old wineskin—Luke 5:37–39.
Satan entered into Judas—Luke 22:3; John 13:2.
House cleansed of leaven—Exod. 12:15; Mishnah, Pesachim 1:1.

Chapter 6: Premonitions

Story of Mary and Martha—Luke 10:38–42.

Diatribe against scribes and Pharisees—Matt. 23:13–36.

Man carrying a jar of water—Mark 14:13–14; Luke 22:10–13.

Jesus prepares to eat the Passover—Matt. 26:17–18; Mark 14:12–16; Luke 22:8.

Parable of the soil—Matt. 13:3–23; Mark 4:2–20; Luke 8:5–15.

Mary could have heard the parable of the soil—Matt. 12:46; Mark 3:31–32; Luke 8:19-20.

Jesus' friendship with Mary, Martha, and Lazarus—John 11:5.

Chapter 7: Sacrifice

Messianic expectation—Isa. 11:1–5.

Andrew brings Peter to Jesus, the Messiah—John 1:40–42.

Passage in Isaiah—"Spirit of God is upon him"—Isa. 61:1–2.

Jesus reads in Nazareth synagogue—Luke 4:16–21.

Attempt on Jesus' life in Nazareth—Luke 4:28–30.

Martha's statement of faith, that Jesus is the Christ—John 11:25–27.

Ritual of Passover sacrifice—Mishnah, Pesachim 5:6.

Chapter 8: Passover

Passover—Exodus 12:3–20; Mishnah, Pesachim 10:5

No passover feast leftovers—Exodus 34:25..

Hallel—Ps. 113–118.

Great Hallel—Ps. 136.

Chapter 9: Surrender

Jesus institutes communion—Matt. 26:26–29; Mark 14:22–24; Luke 22:17–20.

Announcement of betrayal—Matt. 26:21; Mark 14:18; Luke 22:21.
"Who is greatest?"—Luke 22:24.
Disciple first called—John 1:35–40.
Foot washing—John 13:2–15.
Discourse—John 13:12–16:33.
Prayer—John 17.
Gethsemane—Mark 14:32–42; Luke 22:39–46; John 18:1–11.
Disciples fall asleep—Matt. 26:36–46; Mark 14:37–42.

Chapter 10: Condemnation
Arrest—Matt. 26:50.
Annas sees prisoner first—John 18:13, 19–24.
Jesus taken to Caiaphas—Matt. 26:57; John 18:24.
False witnesses—Matt. 26:60; Mark 14:56.
John known to high priest—John 18:15–16.
Peter's denial—Matt. 26:69–75; Mark 14:66–72; Luke 22:55–62; John 18:17–18, 25–27.
Jesus' "confession" of who he is—Matt. 26:64; Luke 22:70.
Judas returns the silver—Matt. 27:3–5.
Judas hangs himself—Matt. 27:5.
Betrayal money used to purchase burial field for strangers—Matt. 27:7.

Chapter 11: Trial
Jesus before Pilate—Matt. 27:11–26; Mark 15:2–15; Luke 23:1–6, 11; John 18:28–19:16.
Jesus before Herod—Luke 23:7–11.
Jesus before Pilate the second time—Luke 23:11, 13–25.
Claudia's dream and warning—Matt. 27:19.
Mock coronation—Matt. 27:27–30; Mark 15:16–19.

Chapter 12: Agony

Mary Magdalene—seven demons—Luke 8:2.
Simon of Cyrene—Matt. 27:32; Mark 15:21; Luke 23:26.
Daughters of Jerusalem—Luke 23:28–31.
Crucifixion—Matt. 27:33–50; Mark 15:22–37; Luke 23:32–46; John 19:25–37.
Friends around the cross—Matt. 27:55–56; Mark 15:40–41; Luke 23:49; John 19:25–26.
Centurion's remark—Matt. 27:54; Mark 15:39; Luke 23:47.
Burial of bodies before dark—Deut. 21:22–23.
Simeon's prediction—Luke 2:35

Chapter 13: Reminiscence

Joseph of Arimathea—Matt. 27:57–60; Mark 15:42–46; Luke 23:50–53.
Also Nicodemus—John 19:38–42.
Jesus at twelve years of age—Luke 2:41–51.
Anna and Simeon—Luke 2:25–38.
Gabriel's words to Mary, "He will be great"—Luke 1:32.
Isaiah—child born to sit on David's throne—Isa. 9:6–7.
An angel visits Joseph in a dream—Matt. 1:20–21.
Micah—king from Bethlehem—Mic. 5:2.
Jesus quotes Isaiah in Nazareth—Luke 4:18-19.
Isaiah—eyes of the blind… dumb sing for joy—Isa. 35:5–6.
Isaiah—"come forth a shoot"—Isa. 11:1–2.
Zechariah—"king comes to you… foal of an ass"—Zech. 9:9.
Isaiah—Jesus' torture—Isa. 53:1–9.
Shedding of blood for forgiveness of sins—Heb. 9:13–14.

Chapter 14: Joy

Women at the tomb—composite of Matt. 28:1–7; Mark 16:1–8; Luke 24:1–11; John 20:1, 11–18.
Peter and John at the tomb—John 20:2–9.
Caesarea Philippi—Matt. 16:13–17.

Messianic revelation—Matt. 16:16; Mark 8:29–30.
Meeting of disciples after resurrection—Luke 24:33; John 20:19.
Cleopas and one other on road to Emmaus—Luke 24:13–35.
Jesus appears to gathering of disciples—Luke 24:36–49; John 20:19–29.

Printed in the United States
202548BV00004B/1-6/A